"Your timing is impeccable…"

Cori continued, "I was just thinking about you." At once she noticed how good he looked with scruffy facial hair, a gray button-down shirt open at the neck and those tight black jeans. His mere presence made her reconsider those silly friendship thoughts.

"In a good way, I hope." Gage's grin grew wider, and his dark eyes sparkled under the glow of the streetlights.

"I thought you were ignoring me."

"I was, and I'm sorry about that. My grandfather is a powerful force, but he finally went up to his room," he said.

"Is this a vacation?"

"It's more of an attempt at reconnecting my family."

"Sounds as if you burned a lot of bridges."

"More like I soaked them in gasoline and used a flamethrower."

"I'm getting a little worried." Cori smiled.

"About what?"

"About us."

"Things are looking up. I didn't know we were an *us*." Gage laughed.

She chuckled an[d]   [m]ake
her intentions cle[ar]

"That all depend[s]

Dear Reader,

The inspiration for this book arrived like a thunderstorm on the prairie, all at once and with a charging force. At first I didn't know if I could craft it in such a way that I wouldn't find myself simply extolling the wonders of Zane Grey, but as I kept plotting and honing the story, the heroine and hero came to life. Not only are they real to me, but their plight has personal resonance.

I grew up surrounded by several relatives who abused alcohol, and I know firsthand what it means to watch someone you love drift away from you. I wanted to show how Gage, the hero of this story, lost his cowboy ways, but with the help of his sometimes grumpy grandfather, a beautiful, feisty doctor and her sweet daughter, along with the cowboy values that encompass the works of Zane Grey, Gage just might save himself before it's too late.

The time I spent in Durango for the annual Zane Grey West Society's conference was a real treat. I based a lot of my scenes on the actual conference, but this is a work of fiction, and as such, I took some liberties with the events of the conference and the actual establishments in Durango. That being said, the Strater Hotel, the Narrow Gauge Railroad and Museum, and the historic mining town of Silverton are very real and make for a great family vacation.

Please visit me at maryleo.com, where you'll find some fun facts about old-time cowboys, the Zane Grey West Society and Durango. While you're there you might want to sign up for my newsletter. You can also find me on Facebook and Twitter @maryleoauthor, where we can chat.

Happy trails,

Mary

HER FAVORITE COWBOY

MARY LEO

HARLEQUIN® AMERICAN ROMANCE®

Recycling programs
for this product may
not exist in your area.

ISBN-13: 978-0-373-75585-1

Her Favorite Cowboy

Copyright © 2015 by Mary Leo

Printed in U.S.A.

USA TODAY bestselling author **Mary Leo** grew up in south Chicago in the tangle of a big Italian family. She's worked in Hollywood, Las Vegas and in Silicon Valley. Currently she lives in San Diego with her husband, author Terry Watkins, and their sweet kitty, Sophie. Visit her website at maryleo.com.

Books by Mary Leo

Harlequin American Romance

Falling for the Cowboy
Aiming for the Cowboy
Christmas with the Rancher

For Henry and Catherine Nardi, who introduced me to the many books of Zane Grey, and for inviting us to our first annual Zane Grey West Society's conference. The time spent at those conferences, both in your company and in the company of so many wonderful people, has truly been life-changing. Thank you!

Chapter One

"I'll get the bags," Gage Remington told his grandpa Buck as he pulled into the last available parking spot. On any other occasion Gage would never drive his expensive car over gravel and dirt, but he'd spent the past thirty minutes trying his best to find parking in town and he was at his wits' end. Gravel would have to do.

"Don't be treating me like I'm an invalid," Buck said, as he swung open the passenger door on the black Mercedes. "Just 'cause you ain't seen me for the past five years, don't mean I deteriorated into some feeble old man. There might be snow on my roof, but there's still a fire burning inside. I can roll a dang suitcase up the sidewalk."

"It's your call, Grandpa. I was just offering."

"Thanks, but I'm fine."

It had been a stressful drive into Durango from Albuquerque, New Mexico, the closest town with a major airport, where they'd met to drive in together. It had taken four long hours and Gage was already second-guessing his decision to spend some quality time with his grandfather.

Gage had worshiped his grandfather when he was a kid, and had spent three weeks every summer with his grandparents on their ranch just outside of Briggs, Idaho, a quirky little town that Gage had loved. It had been the single event he'd looked forward to all year long. His grandma always said they were like two peas in a pod. That Gage was simply a younger version of his gramps. Gage had loved the comparison and tried his best to imitate his gramps.

Not only had his grandfather taught him how to saddle up and ride a horse, but he would spend hours teaching him how to do a chore the proper way, how to be patient with a bucking horse, how to listen to someone's complaint with an open heart and how to suck it up when something unfortunate happened. He shared his beliefs that the common folks had the ability to change a society for the good, that the rising tide lifted all boats, and that you never asked a cowboy to ride a horse you wouldn't ride yourself. But the one truth Gage remembered most was how "sometimes it takes something bad to happen to a person before that person can bring out his best."

When Gage was a kid, his grandfather's wisdom hadn't always meant much, but now, after everything he'd gone through in recent months, Gage wasn't so sure his best would be good enough.

He wished he had spent more summers on the ranch, but once he'd gotten into college and later graduated, he landed a high-paying job on Wall Street. Soon after, he'd gotten married and begun moving up the corporate ladder. There wasn't any time to visit his grandparents. Even when his sweet grandmother passed away two years ago, he hadn't been able to make the funeral due to all his obligations, a decision that still haunted him.

He had been all set to go, even bought the plane tickets for himself and his wife, but then at the last minute his boss had offered him his weekly spot with Tricia Massey, dispensing *Wall Street Wisdom* to her millions of fans. His boss had had a conflicting obligation and was depending on him to step in with Ms. Massey on her TV show. Gage had talked it over with his wife and concluded it was the chance of a lifetime to take his career to the next level, so he simply couldn't pass it up.

His grandfather never quite forgave him.

Now Gage was trying his best to rekindle that shredded bond and make it up to him. So far, it didn't seem to be working. Ever since his grandma had passed, his grandfather had turned into a recluse with attitude. Gage knew this trip would be difficult.

He never imagined it would be impossible.

Gage slipped out of the car, and popped open the trunk. Before he could say another word Buck had pulled out his suitcase, tugged up the handle and was headed for the Strater Hotel a block away, leaving Gage in his dust…literally.

Not only were his black jeans now covered in white powder, but a pickup truck had sped through the lot, shooting up stones and dust that now covered Gage from head to toe. Even his new cowboy hat, which he'd carefully placed on top of the suitcases in the trunk, showed a fine sprinkling of white.

"You go on ahead, Gramps. I'll be right behind you," Gage yelled to the spunky older man who had somehow managed to get to the sidewalk before the pickup had roared through the lot.

His grandfather never turned around or acknowledged Gage. He just kept walking toward the hotel.

"Fine," Gage mumbled to himself, then slammed the trunk closed without taking out his bags. No way did he want to go up to the room with Gramps to get settled in. "Oh, yeah, this was a good idea. What the heck was I thinking?"

He locked the doors and headed down the street, some twenty-five feet behind his grandfather, grateful they were no longer stuck together in the car. For the past four hours they'd barely spoken, and when they had, Gramps disagreed with just about everything, even the type of gas Gage should use in his own car.

What he needed now was some time away from him at a bar—preferably a crowded bar—to make him forget that he was spending the next two weeks with the man.

In the same hotel.

In the same room.

Attending the same convention.

Thankfully the convention only lasted a few days. After that, instead of "seeing the sights," they could each return home if they so chose. And if Gage had anything to say about it, they would leave tonight.

Gage walked toward the Strater Hotel, which happened to be located in the historic section of downtown Durango, Colorado. Fortunately, right there on the bottom floor of the grand old red Victorian brick hotel and seemingly not connected to the lobby where his grandfather was no doubt dutifully checking in, was a noisy old-time saloon named The Diamond Belle.

As soon as Gage approached the entrance, the sound of honky-tonk piano filled his ears. He opened the screen door to discover a large crowded room with agreeable-looking people enjoying a late afternoon fermented beverage.

Gage had stopped drinking alcohol six months ago, right after his wife had asked him for a divorce. He still longed to partake, but knew he would merely enjoy the atmosphere of a tavern and save the hard liquor for some other time.

The mix of familiar sounds and smells put a smile on Gage's otherwise weary face as he entered the colorful old-time room.

He immediately made his way to the one open spot at the impressive oak bar and ordered a tall glass of soda water with three limes from a male bartender who looked a lot like he'd just stepped out of a Western movie.

"Been a long day?" a woman with raven hair that curled down her back sitting on the barstool next to him asked.

"Way too long," he said without really looking at her. He wasn't exactly in the mood for small talk.

The bartender delivered his drink and Gage guzzled half of it down.

"Well, at least it's over," the woman told him, her voice low and sexy.

He placed the glass down on the cocktail napkin and turned to face her, thinking he'd find a way to brush her off and move on down the crowded bar to a better spot where he wouldn't be required to speak.

As soon as he saw her face, his stomach tensed and he knew his ability to ignore her would be difficult. Not only was she beautiful, with that silky hair caressing her lovely face and those amazing gray eyes staring up at him, but she had a smile that changed his mind about walking away.

Instead, he said, "Actually, it's only just begun."

"Something you still have to do?"

"Two weeks' worth of somethings."

"Ouch! That's a long time to be miserable."

He needed some sympathy at the moment, and this goddess in blue jeans seemed to be saying all the right words.

"Might be, but for now, sitting here talking to you, I'm feeling a whole lot better."

He hoped she would stick around for a while, at least until he finished his soda. She was easy on the eyes, and after staring at his grandfather's sourpuss face for the past several hours Gage could feel his disposition changing for the better.

"Glad I could help," she said, her voice enticing enough to make him imagine things he shouldn't be thinking about. Especially since he'd made a promise to himself to steer clear of women until he figured out what the heck he wanted to do with his life now that his divorce was officially final.

It had been one of those messy divorces and had caught him completely off guard. They had been talking about having a baby and buying a bigger place when his wife of four years had sprung it on him during a dinner party at her parents' house. She confessed that she had fallen out of love with him and "didn't like who he'd become," as her dad plated the pot roast. Her two older brothers and their wives were seated around the table as she made clear her intentions. His wife had never liked to do anything major without her family present, and announcing that she wanted to jettison her marriage had apparently been one of those major moments.

Needless to say, the dinner hadn't gone well after that, at which her mom had literally cried, not because of the pending divorce, but because she had worked all day in the kitchen preparing the perfect pot roast and a seven-layer cake that was "to die for."

The memory of that dinner party still stung as Gage

watched the woman on the bar stool next to him flip her silky hair over a shoulder and blink those steel-gray eyes, as a warm smile creased her seductive red lips.

Oh, yeah, she was way too easy on the eyes.

He drank down more of his soda and once again thought about moving to another spot. And once again she changed his mind.

"You have no idea."

"How so?"

He wanted to tell her all about his recent divorce and his voluntary extended leave from his lucrative nine-to-five to go on some misguided nostalgic trip with his grandfather in order to reconnect with his youth. But getting into the details of his sordid life was not something he had ever enjoyed doing.

Instead, Gage switched his thoughts back to his grandfather. "I'm thinking the relationship might improve if I try a little harder."

"By 'relationship,' are you talking about a relationship with a woman?"

Gage shook his head. "No. I'm through with women for a while." He sucked in a deep breath and slowly let it out. "What I mean to say is, my main focus at the moment is on rebuilding a relationship with my grandfather."

She took a sip of her red wine, and he noticed her dark red manicured nails. They screamed city girl.

"I take it that's not working out either."

He shook his head. "Not really. He hates me, and I'm beginning to think he has just cause. I haven't been a very good grandson lately."

"How so?"

Gage stared into those big eyes of hers. "You cut right to the chase, don't you?"

"Only because you seem to want to talk about it."

He hesitated. Baring his soul had never been easy for him and he wasn't about to start stripping for a stranger, albeit a beautiful, intuitive stranger.

"Maybe some other time."

"So you don't want to talk about it?"

"Not really. No."

She smiled. "I'd ask you if there was any way I could help, but under the circumstances, you may get the wrong idea."

He chuckled. "What, you mean because you're sitting on a bar stool, and you're offering me comfort?"

"Exactly."

He leaned into the bar and turned toward her, a smirk on his face. "Okay, if it's not *that* kind of comfort then tell me what you're offering?

"A shoulder to cry on. Sometimes it helps to vent. No judgment or advice involved."

He gazed at her shoulders covered in the crisp white cotton shirt that hugged her petite body, black hair tumbling down the front of her, hiding full breasts, and a delicate gold necklace fastened around her neck sporting a rather large square-cut ruby. He wondered if the ruby had been a gift or if she'd bought it for herself. Either way, it told him she liked the finer things in life. It was a trait his ex-wife lived for and had kept him addicted to, making more and more money for the entire four years they were married.

"I wouldn't want to get those pretty shoulders of yours all wet," he told her.

"It's a warm day. A little moisture might cool things off a bit."

"Are you always this friendly to strangers, or am I the exception?"

"You have kind eyes. Makes me think you're a good man."

"Not very. People I love seem to end up hating me."

"Hate's a strong word." She sipped her wine. "You're too charming for anyone to hate you."

A great big grin captured her face and he about melted. The woman was all allure and style…too bad he wasn't interested. This trip was about his finding his soul again, rekindling a relationship with his grandfather, going back to his roots, remaining sober and deciding what he really wanted out of life. Those were the important things.

It most certainly was not about hooking up with a captivating woman he'd met in a bar.

"You don't know me. I could be a terrible person."

"A little misguided perhaps, but definitely not terrible."

"How can you be so sure?

"It's right there in your eyes. Besides, I'm a good judge of character."

Gage turned his back to the bar, to get a better look at his judge in cowgirl boots. "And what kind of character do you see in me?"

"It's your demeanor, and the fact that you're covered in dust. I'd say you just parked in the dirt parking lot behind this hotel. You seem a bit shaky, so I'm going to guess you're coming off a long drive with your grandfather. And, for some reason, you and he have a strained relationship that you're trying to mend, thus the sparkling water and not a beer or something stronger to hamper your reactions. That makes you a stand-up kind of guy."

Gage was stunned. "What are you, some kind of psychic or something?"

She laughed. "Not exactly, I just went through almost the same experience with my grandmother. Note the dust on my boots."

She held out her leg, and sure enough her brown cowgirl boots were covered in a thin coating of white dust.

She said, "I take it you and your grandfather are here for the Zane Grey convention?"

He knocked off the rest of his soda and asked the bartender for another. "We sure are."

"First time?"

"Yep. Been hearing about this convention for more years than I can remember. Read most every book the man ever wrote. Had to. Gramps wouldn't let me ride Smokey, my favorite horse, if I didn't read at least four chapters every day during the summers I visited him. Those were some of the best times of my childhood."

"Same here, only it wasn't for a ride on a horse. My grandma made the absolute best cakes and cookies in the entire world, and she wouldn't teach me how to make them unless I could discuss one of Zane's books while we baked. My mom and I would visit her every summer for an entire month. Some of my best memories are tied up with that woman." She held out her hand. "Cori Parker. And you are?"

He took her hand in his, and at once he felt a burning heat slip through his body. He quickly let go.

"Gage Remington, grandson to Buck Remington, a cantankerous old cowboy who is up in our room right now, undoubtedly charting out how to make my life a living hell for the next two weeks…which I fully deserve."

She snickered. "I'm sure that's not the case. If he's anything like my grandmother, Miss May Meriwether, he's too busy reacquainting himself with friends."

Cori nodded toward a group of older folks sitting around a couple of small tables in the corner, obviously enjoying themselves. Their laughter permeated the entire saloon.

Unfortunately for Gage, his grandfather was not one of them.

Cori continued. "She's the petite lady, wearing jeans and a blue shirt. She's the only one with brown hair. Gram turns seventy-five next week, but she's fighting it as long as she can."

"My grandfather was like that. Always took care of himself, but ever since my grandmother passed, he's been nothing but…"

An older, slim man wearing a black cowboy hat rushed into the saloon from the open back door and yelled, "Is anyone in here a nurse or a doctor?"

The music stopped as the room took on a sudden eerie silence. Everyone collectively waited for someone to respond to the frantic question.

A few awkward seconds passed.

Then Gage watched as Cori slid off her barstool, grabbed her oversize purse, and said, "I'm a doctor."

The man told her to follow him, which she did, as she reached out for Gage's hand. He reluctantly took it and followed close behind.

"You're a doctor?" Gage asked her as they made their way out of the tavern area. He never would have guessed. He always thought of doctors as older, wiser-looking people. Not someone he could meet in a bar, and especially not someone who looked and sounded like Cori Parker, with her sultry voice, tight jeans, boots and manicured fingernails. She simply didn't fit the type, but then, what did he know of types? He hadn't looked up from achieving his financial goals in way too many years.

"Yes," she said. "And I need you as my assistant."

"But I don't know the first thing about…"

"Just follow my lead and you'll do fine."

She squeezed his hand tighter as if she was depending on him for strength. He quickly took up the cause, gaining confidence with each step, and followed her through the back of the saloon, which led directly into the lobby of the Strater Hotel.

As he and Cori came around the corner, past the wooden staircase and into the main lobby decorated with crystal chandeliers, wallpapered walls, antique walnut furniture and ornate woodwork, he spotted the man lying on the plush, carpeted floor in the center of a small group of people who knelt around him.

Gage's heart raced as he let go of Cori's hand and hurried toward the group.

"It's my grandfather," he told Cori, his voice cracking.

"I DON'T KNOW what happened," the young man told Cori as he crouched next to the older man lying on the floor. "One minute he was standing in front of my desk getting his room key, and the next he was on the floor."

A small group of older folks had gathered around the gray-haired man lying on the floor. Cori immediately focused on the color of the man's skin, which looked normal, plus his eyes were open and he wasn't clutching his chest.

All good signs.

"Oh, Gramps," Gage whispered as he dropped to the floor next to the fallen man. Then he smoothed out his grandpa's hair, which seemed to relax them both.

As soon as his grandfather heard Gage's voice he turned toward him. "What? How did I ever get on the floor?" He sounded shaky, deliberate, as if he was trying to control internal tremors. Cori knew these symptoms well, but she didn't want to jump to any conclusions. It was always difficult coming into a situation like she now found herself. She longed for a patient who filled out a medical history. Just once she'd like to know what that was like. Even though she had worked in a low trauma hospital in Manhattan as an ER physician, her experience with a detailed medical history for any of her patients had been a rare luxury, rather than the norm.

"Do you know if he's suffering from any blood sugar problems?" Cori asked Gage as she clocked the man's pulse. She could feel his tremors as she held on to his wrist. He also seemed anxious and nervous, but that could be from what had to be an embarrassing situation.

Gage hesitated as Cori looked to him for an easy answer. His grandfather was breathing too fast, which would only make him dizzy.

"I don't know."

"He's your grandfather. Do you know anything about his health?"

"No. Not really."

His statements took her by surprise, especially since he'd claimed to want to spend time with his grandfather.

Cori knew everything about her grandmother, down to what vitamins she took and what she ate for breakfast. But then, Cori had always shared a special relationship with her gram, and felt closer to her than she did to her own parents.

"What's his name?"

"Buck, Buck Remington."

Cori directed her full attention to the patient. "Mr. Remington, I'd like you to take some deep, slow breaths to calm yourself. Can you do that for me? I'll lead the way?"

Buck nodded, as they each slowly sucked in air through their mouths. "Now let it out through your nose," she told him, and he dutifully followed her lead.

Once she had him breathing normally, his pulse slowed to a more acceptable pace. An older woman with pure white, shoulder-length hair and deep red lips leaned over and handed Gage her pink sweater. "Maybe you can put this under his head. That floor's hard."

"Thanks," Gage told her, while Cori threw the generous woman a quick smile.

Gage looked to Cori for approval. She nodded, then he carefully lifted Buck's head and rested it on the folded sweater.

"Have you been diagnosed with hypoglycemia, Mr. Remington?"

He nodded again. His pulse quickened and sweat beaded on his forehead.

She looked up at Gage. "He needs glucose. Could you get him a glass of orange juice from the bar?"

"Sure." Gage jumped up and rushed back to the tavern.

"I caught him as he went down," a tall, lean gentleman, probably in his late sixties or early seventies and wearing a cream-colored cowboy hat offered. "He didn't hit anything but my chest, so nothing should be broken. Court's the name. Steve Court. Been Buck's friend for the past ten years or so. Never know'd him to drop like that. Glad I was close by to break his fall."

"You did perfect," she told the man, then directed her attention back to Mr. Remington. "Can you sit up?"

He nodded and she motioned for Mr. Court to please help her.

She cradled his head and shoulder with one arm, and Mr. Court leaned down to help put Buck upright.

Gage returned with the juice.

"Drink this, Mr. Remington. It'll make you feel better."

Buck did as he was told and quickly slurped up all the juice, then handed the empty glass back to Gage. "Thank you, son," he mumbled, his hand visibly shaking.

A siren screamed in the distance.

"Don't worry, Gramps. We'll get you checked out at the hospital, and you'll be fine."

"I'm not going to no dang hospital. I'm fine now. Just lost my balance is all."

He struggled with each movement as if his limbs wouldn't cooperate with his mind.

"Just rest for a bit, Mr. Remington. Take your time. There's no rush."

"Not going to no dang hospital."

Two male EMTs walked into the lobby and came over to the group. The glow of the swirling red lights from their ambulance pulsed in through the windows and stained the walls with their fiery color.

"Gramps, stop being so obstinate. I'll be right there with you."

"You ain't been with me since you was a kid. Don't

think you can tell me what to do now. I can make my own decisions."

Cori quickly realized their relationship was in even worse shape than Gage had led her to believe.

She reached out and took Mr. Remington's hand. "I knew a Buck when I was in medical school. He was a kind, thoughtful, easy-going man. I think those traits go along with the name. I have a feeling you probably didn't eat a meal for a long time, and because of that, you might not be your sweet self. Your grandson only wants what's best for you, and so do I."

Buck nodded, staring into Cori's eyes. His demeanor changed and Cori could see the tension drain from his body. He relaxed his shoulders, and gently squeezed her hand.

Cori worked on instinct and purposely stopped herself from thinking about what she was doing or saying despite the fact that she had started second-guessing herself a few months back.

Her self-doubt and stress had caused her to walk away from her ER position at Manhattan Central Hospital for some much-needed rest and reassessment. She'd been chronically fatigued for weeks from lack of sleep. And after nearly running off the road with her nine-year-old daughter Hailey in the car on their way home from another school event that Cori had all but missed, she knew her life had to change.

Those changes began with her turning in her resignation.

Up until that moment, Cori had thought she could do it all. Now she wasn't so sure she could do anything right, and that included diagnosing hypoglycemia in an elderly man with the appropriate symptoms.

She gazed at her patient and saw all the fear and loneliness in his light blue eyes.

He couldn't seem to stop staring at her, as if he was trying to place where he'd seen her before, but Cori knew that wasn't possible.

"Rose? What are you doing here, Rose? I thought you were…"

"My name is Cori, Mr. Remington. I'm not Rose."

He hesitated for a second, smiled and whispered, "You remind me of my wife. Same color hair and eyes. And your voice, there's something familiar about your voice. She was a looker just like you, and a real spitfire. That woman could get me to eat hay if she asked me to. Always kept me on a schedule. Since she passed, I don't know when to eat or what to eat. I'm all mixed up. It ain't right that she left first. Ain't right at all."

"My grandmother passed a couple years ago," Gage told her.

She understood Buck's despair much better now. She could identify with it.

"It's hard losing someone you love, especially your soul mate. Believe me, I know how you feel. I lost my husband five years ago. He took a piece of my heart that I'll never get back. But he wanted me to go on and be well and love again. I'm sure Rose wanted the same for you. You need to take care of yourself for Rose."

His defenses seemed to tumble down, and she saw only love in his eyes. "She always took good care of me."

"Then don't let her down. Please allow these competent professionals to take you to the hospital to run a few tests. I'm sure it won't take very long, and if everything goes well, your grandson will have you back here in time for the barbecue tonight."

Gage's eyes were moist as he turned to his grandfather. "We'll get you fixed up, Gramps. I'm here now, and I'll see to it that you get everything you need."

"Thanks, son," Buck told him as he allowed one of the EMTs to help him into a wheelchair and roll him out of the lobby.

Cori and Gage stood, and at once she caught a whiff of cinnamon mixed with citrus. Nothing heavy. It was more aromatic than anything else. She gazed around the room, wondering if there was a candle burning or if perhaps there was a plate of cookies on the front desk, but she couldn't see anything.

Gage took her hand in his, running his thumb over the back of her hand. His touch sent a shiver through her.

"Are you always this amazing?" he asked.

"Your grandfather's the one who's amazing. I merely did what I was trained to do."

"Thank you."

She glanced out the front window. The ambulance was getting ready to leave.

"You better get going."

"Will you be here when we get back?"

"All five days."

"Great."

And he took off out the front door, leaving Cori to wonder what exactly he meant by that. Cori hadn't come on this trip with her gram looking for anything other than some time to heal and rethink her chosen profession. Meeting a pseudo cowboy hadn't been part of her idea of healing, and she certainly didn't want to add any complications to her already taxed life.

But still…

Chapter Two

As it turned out, Doctor Cori Parker had been right about Gage's grandfather collapsing from acute hypoglycemia. Other than a low iron count and some arthritis in his joints, Gramps was in excellent health for a man in his seventies. All those years of cowboying had done well by him. Of course, they hadn't done much for his ornery disposition.

"I don't need no rest up in the room," Gramps told Gage in no uncertain terms as they entered the hotel's front lobby once again. "We got ourselves an opening talk and a barbecue to attend. There ain't nothing short of death that's gonna stop me from enjoying every part of this here conference."

Gage decided it was easier to simply roll with the program than to continue arguing his point. "Whatever you say, Gramps. You know best."

His grandfather gave him a little harrumph and moved on ahead of Gage in the direction of the Henry Strater Theater where the event had been planned. By now everyone would be in line for what was sure to be a Western treat with some fine Colorado beef, chicken and all the trimmings for a real down-home kind of meal, something Gage hadn't experienced in too many years to remember. His ex-wife's parents had come close several times, but a pot roast was little substitution for a rack of ribs and grilled chicken.

Gage tried to keep up, but his grandfather seemed to want to prove that he was "fit as a fiddle," a saying his gramps liked to use, and had already disappeared around the corner of the lobby. In truth, now that his gramps was feeling better, with no side-effects from his collapse, all Gage could think about was Cori Parker. She'd been on his mind ever since he'd met her, and despite all his efforts to shake her free, he seemed to be stuck wanting to see her again, if for nothing else but to thank her for taking such good care of his grandfather.

But that had to be it.

He'd thank her and let it go at that.

Nothing more.

There would be no getting involved no matter how intoxicating her eyes were, or the sultry curve of her lips, or the way she had soothed his worries when his grandfather was in crisis.

He reminded himself that she was merely doing her job. Something she'd been trained to do. His grandfather could have been any number of people in need and the treatment would have been exactly the same. Sure, she'd been extra kind and compassionate when she learned about his grandmother's passing, but weren't all doctors trained to be empathetic to the elderly?

He tried to think of her as just another doctor when he spotted her standing in front of the open doors to the theater. With one glance, his breath caught in his throat, and his stomach was clenched.

"What the—" he said under his breath, angry that he'd had such a visceral reaction. He shook the sensation free, and forced his now-tense body to relax as he watched his grandfather give her a tight hug. One thing was for sure—the men in his family sure took to her like bees to honey.

He stopped walking and chided himself for the analogy. He hadn't been in the west for more than a day and already his thoughts had gone all folksy.

"You saved my life," Gage overheard Grandpa Buck say when he and Cori separated. His face glowed with appreciation.

"Hardly," Cori told him, a slight blush on her cheeks. "All I did was help you get through a challenging time. Your grandson did much more than I did."

Gage walked up alongside them and immediately his pulse quickened, as if her mere presence caused a physical reaction, which he knew couldn't be the case. They barely knew each other. He blamed his response on the tensions of the day. There could be no other reason… at least none that made any sense.

"It was a good start," Gramps teased, leaning in closer to Cori as if they had a secret bond. There was a time when he and his grandfather had their own secret bond, when his grandfather had a dry sense of humor that Gage always got, and most times added to the joke. Now he questioned almost everything his grandfather said. Nothing seemed funny and everything seemed like an attack.

"Was that a compliment?" Gage asked, hoping his gramps would lighten up.

Grandpa Buck turned to face him. "No. It was a fact." Then he turned and walked into the theater where he met up with some of his male friends, each giving him a strong handshake and a pat on the back. Gage watched as his grandfather's face lit up with each touch, with each recognition, and he longed for that light to be directed in his direction.

"He'll come around. These things take time," Cori said in a low voice.

It was as if Cori could read his mind. "Did anyone ever tell you that you're a little spooky?"

"How so?"

"Do you always know what a person's thinking, or am I one of the lucky ones?"

"You have an expressive face."

"I'll try to keep that in mind whenever you and I are conversing." Gage purposely relaxed the muscles in his face and tried to look deadpan.

She pointed her index finger and made little air circles around his face. He loved being this close to her and seeing her smile. He really worked at remaining expressionless, but as her smile spread, and her perfume engulfed his senses, he couldn't keep a straight face.

"See, right there." She pointed to his eyes, then to his forehead. "And right there. I can tell you're happy to see me. And you want to sit with me during dinner."

"Yes, I'm happy to see you, but I hadn't thought about seating arrangements."

She turned to walk inside. "Well, you should have. I'm a great dinner partner."

He followed close behind, softly chuckling at how she could wrap him around her finger with a few words and a smile. "Let me grab my grandfather and we'll join you at one of the more private tables along the wall. Will that work?"

"Sure, I'll hunt down my family and let them know. There'll be three of us."

Gage left her at the door wondering what she'd meant by her family. He'd thought she had come with her grandmother and no one else, but then, they really hadn't had time to discuss much of anything before his grandfather collapsed in the lobby. A fact that still haunted him. Grandpa Buck could have hit his head on a table or a chair or broken a leg or an arm and where was his grandson?

In a bar…as usual.

THE HENRY STRATER THEATER, according to the brochure Cori had read up in her room, was one of the oldest continually running theaters in Colorado, featuring comedy nights with world-renowned comedians, improv troupes and ragtime music—from *The Rocky Horror Picture Show* during late October to Breakfast with Santa in December. The theater acted as both a community space and a cultural center.

Deep red velvet drapes hung in various areas around the large room and across the stage. Elevated box seats adorned both sides of the room, and exposed redbrick walls gave off an Old West ambience. At once Cori felt as if she'd been transported into another time. A feeling of absolute delight filled her as she walked toward her grandmother and Hailey, her precocious daughter. At one point she had doubted her decision to quit her job.

She wanted a calmer place and a better way to live. She'd thought they could move to her grandmother's small town, until she saw just how small the town really was. There wasn't an adequate local school for Hailey, and the nearest possible employment for Cori was over sixty miles away in Denver.

As soon as they had arrived at her grandmother's

new home, she thought for sure she wouldn't be able to last a week. Her gram had sold the big rambling house soon after Cori's grandpa had died three years ago, and the new one was so small the guest bedroom barely held a double bed and a dresser. The place was great for her gram, but not so great for Cori and Hailey if their visit wasn't going to be a short one.

So many good memories had been centered in her gram's town that Cori had built it up to be somewhat magical. In reality, it was still a sweet little place, but unless she was an entrepreneur or was willing to make the commute into Denver, there was no way she and Hailey could settle there. She would have to find an alternative.

Cori knew she wanted to raise Hailey in a close-knit community—just not her gram's community, which had turned out to be very disappointing for Cori. The thought of not being able to put down roots next to her gram had thrown Cori off course, but hanging out in Durango was proving to be something else entirely. More and more she felt sure this change was exactly what she needed, especially seeing the group of seniors who had gathered in the theater for the buffet-style barbecue dinner during the opening talks of the conference. Cori knew there had to be something more to life than merely working eight to twelve hours a day. She wanted time to spend with her daughter, time to pursue a hobby, time to learn how to cook something other than a prepackaged meal.

There was something comforting about being around energetic older folks, as if they were clearing the path with their tenacity and courage of conviction, saying,

"Look at me! If I can make it to my golden years and still pursue my hobbies and dreams, so can you."

"Mom! Mom! Grammy's going to let me help during the auction. I get to hand out books and stuff. Doesn't that sound like fun?" Hailey's face glowed with anticipation, causing her blue-gray eyes to sparkle. Her thick caramel colored hair was pulled back in a long ponytail, and it bounced with her every move. She wore jeans, a soft pink Western shirt and cowgirl boots Cori hadn't seen before. Obviously, Gram had taken her shopping, a pastime they both enjoyed more than they should.

Hailey could barely contain her excitement. For the most part, she loved doing things with her grammy, especially if the two of them could go shopping either before or afterward. Helping Grammy in the kitchen, however, wasn't on Hailey's list of fun activities, especially if it had anything to do with cleaning up.

Helping out with the auction, on the other hand, sounded perfect.

"Are you sure it will be okay?" Cori asked her gram, who was seated at one of the many long tables.

Cori noticed an empty chair right next to her gram, no doubt being saved especially for Cori's arrival.

"Don't be silly, Corina-May. I never would have suggested it if she couldn't do it. Besides, there'll be a couple other people available to help her," Grandma May said. Grandma May always referred to Cori by her birth name, making it a point to tack on the May part, in case anyone had any doubt who Cori was named after.

Cori looked around the crowded room and spotted Gage coming their way.

"I made a new friend today, and I thought we'd sit

with him and his grandfather for dinner. Would you two mind?"

"Nope," Hailey answered, sticking out her chin and shaking her head. "Does your new friend have any kids I could play with?"

"I don't really know, but if he does, he didn't bring them to the conference."

Cori hadn't given any thought to whether or not Gage was a father. Not that it mattered, but he didn't seem like the type. Dads were usually more in tune with family, and Gage seemed completely out of step with that element of his life.

"That's all right," Hailey mumbled, making a frown.

Cori knew that Hailey was lonely for her friends, especially for her best friend, Susan, who she'd spent time with almost every day since they were five. Her decision to quit her job and move halfway across the country to live with Gram for a while was proving to be more of a challenge than she had anticipated, especially for Hailey. Not being able to play with Susan was really hard on her. Once they settled somewhere, Cori felt confident that Hailey would find a new best friend in no time. Till then, the two girls would have to be content to chat on Skype every night.

"I'm sorry, sweetie, I haven't seen any children at this convention, but when we get back to Grammy's house, we'll make a point of getting out there and meeting some. Okay?"

"We'll go to the Community Center and sign you up for a swimming class or gymnastics and you'll meet lots of kids your age," Gram said, trying to assure her.

"But I already know how to swim and I don't like gymnastics. Don't they have anything else?"

"As soon as we get back to my house, we'll walk on over there and see what they offer. You can sign up for anything you want. Okay?"

"Okay," Hailey mumbled, but Cori could tell she wasn't the least bit excited about the prospects. All Hailey really wanted to do was go back home to be with Susan and her friends. It was up to Cori to change her mind…which wasn't going to be easy.

Cori glanced back to see Gage as he approached. Grandma May tilted her head to get a clear view of Gage Remington as he weaved through the group to get to them. A smile creased May's pink lips and her gray eyes lit up as he approached. "Is that your new friend heading our way?"

Cori turned and threw Gage a welcoming smile. He returned the gesture, and his entire face lit up. He was more ruggedly handsome when he smiled, if that was even possible. Cori didn't know if her attraction to him was causing his looks to take on an Adonis flair or if he'd had those qualities from the beginning. Either way, her insides had turned to mush, watching him approach.

"Where'd you find him?" Gram asked.

"In the bar this afternoon."

"He's a real looker. Is he your boyfriend?"

"I just met him. How could he be my boyfriend?"

"It took your grandpa and me about ten minutes to know we were in love. What's taking you so long?"

"Love is something that grows with time." Cori was thinking about Jeremy, her deceased husband. They had known each other for three years before they'd started dating, then another two before they were married, each wanting to be sure marriage was the right move.

"In my day, as soon as you met someone you knew

in that instant whether or not you were in love. I think it has to do with smell. Either you like the way he smells or you don't. What's he smell like?"

"I don't know."

"Sure you do, or he wouldn't be heading our way."

Cori thought about it for a moment and remembered how she had caught a citrusy cinnamon scent when they were in the lobby. That couldn't have been from Gage. Way too sweet to come from a man. Men were more musky, more driftwood and cedar, not lemons and cookies.

"He has no particular scent."

"Hogwash! And why didn't you warn me we would be sitting with your new boyfriend? I would've worn my red lipstick. I look younger with red lips. You don't want him to think your grandmother's old, do you?"

Cori wanted to tell her the truth: *you are old, Gram*, but she knew better.

"Gram, he's just a friend."

Grandma May's demeanor suddenly changed for the worse as she stared past Gage toward the group standing at the end of the buffet line. "Darn. He's back."

"Who?"

"That old coot, Buck Remington. I thought for sure with what happened earlier he'd be out for the entire conference. He's already back, thinking up ways to aggravate me, I'm sure. Couldn't you have insisted they keep him at the hospital for at least twenty-four hours?"

"No, Gram. He's fine. Nothing that a good meal can't fix. And what do you mean by 'old coot?' Buck's a sweetheart."

Cori knew what low blood sugar could do to a person's personality, and Buck was certainly a prime example.

Low blood sugar could change his mood, blur his vision, make it difficult for him to concentrate or make a decision, and cause him to be suddenly excessively hungry. If it ever became severe, like it already had, he would faint, or worse, he could slip into a coma.

"Please don't mention his name in my presence, Corina-May. The man has caused me nothing but grief since the very first moment we met. He's a thorn in my side, and I want nothing to do with him. Ever."

Gage angled up beside Cori, sticking out his hand for Grandma May. "You must be Cori's grandmother. It's so very nice to meet you."

May took his hand in hers, her eyes twinkling with delight, but Cori knew this wouldn't go well once she learned his last name, so she interrupted the name exchange. "Gage, this is my grandmother, May. Gram, this is Gage."

She purposely left out last names, trying her best to avoid a confrontation.

"Nice to meet you, Gage," her grandmother said, a warm smile as big as pie on her friendly face.

"And this is my daughter, Hailey."

Hailey politely stuck out her hand, Gage took it, but Cori could tell he seemed somewhat confused.

"Very nice to meet you," Hailey told him giving him a firm handshake, pumping his hand twice then letting go. Hailey liked to shake hands with the people her mom and grandmother introduced her to. She thought it made her look more grown-up. Cori didn't know if anyone thought she looked more grown-up, but they certainly remembered the little girl who shook their hand.

"And you, as well." He turned to Cori bringing his

voice down low under the din of the voices in the room. "But I thought you were…"

"Single? I am," she whispered. "My husband passed away several years ago."

"I'm so sorry." His face turned solemn, as if he was truly saddened by her loss. Cori appreciated his sympathy, but there were other more pressing issues to be dealt with. "Thanks. We need to talk," Cori said under her breath.

"Where are we moving to?" Gram asked, grabbing her purse off the extra chair.

"Give us a minute," Cori told her, as she caught the glare on Buck's face as he stared over at May, then back at Cori. And in that instant, the situation must have registered and he called out to Gage.

Gage held up a finger, asking him to wait. Buck wanted no part of waiting. He headed straight for his grandson, his scowl growing with each step. Apparently, the animosity that had poured from Grandma May was mutual.

"I think we have a grandparent problem," Cori told Gage as her grandmother finally caught on to the situation. She immediately plopped right back down in her chair, folded her arms across her chest and waited for Buck to approach.

"What kind of grandparent problem?"

"The kind that means we won't be sharing a meal tonight or most likely any night during this conference if they have their way."

"Why not? Did I say something wrong?"

"It has nothing to do with you. I think…"

Buck interrupted. "Son, if you want to keep me as

your grandfather and not have me disown you completely, you'll step away from that there table."

He turned to Cori. "Are you related to that woman?" He nodded toward May.

"'That woman' is my grandmother," Cori said.

"That's most unfortunate."

"Gramps, Cori saved your life today. You said so yourself."

"And for that, I'm grateful, but as long as you're related to *that woman*," he tilted his head in May's direction, "I don't want anything to do with you. C'mon, son, we need to get us some seats as far away from this table as possible."

And he marched off with a loud *harrumph*.

Gage ran a hand through his thick hair and shuffled his feet. "I don't know what this is all about, but I'm sure going to find out. That was totally out of line and I'm sorry. Maybe he just needs some food and he'll calm down."

"That old coot ain't never going to calm down," Grandma May warned. "He was born ornery." She turned to Cori. "You don't want no part of a Remington, Corina-May. They're nothing but trouble. Hailey and me are getting in the dinner line before all the good stuff's gone. Are you coming?"

"I'll be right there, Gram. You guys go on ahead."

She stormed off with the same loud *harrumph* that Buck used. Hailey glanced at her mom, gave her a weak smile, shrugged and then followed her grandmother.

"Do you understand any of this?" Gage asked Cori.

"No. I've never seen my grandmother so upset. She's usually happy and loves everyone she meets. This is crazy."

"I wish I could say the same for my grandfather. Unfortunately, grumpy seems to be his only gear."

Cori chuckled. "It's been a long day for everyone. Maybe we should keep our distance until we find out what this is all about."

She secretly wanted him to stay and tell her the heck with their grandparents, the three of them would sit at their own table. But instead he agreed. "Probably a good idea."

Then, without so much as a smile or a "see ya later," Gage hurried to catch up with his grandfather, leaving Cori to wonder if there was more to his hasty departure than merely wanting to please his grandfather.

IT NEVER OCCURRED to Gage that Cori could have a child... Not that she didn't seem like the type... It was more that in his circles none of his friends had children or even mentioned children. They weren't on his radar screen, so he never imagined himself as father material.

He and his ex-wife had discussed it briefly when they were married, right before she'd asked for a divorce, but for the most part raising a family had been pushed off into the future...the distant future. He always thought he wasn't cut out to be someone's dad. Way too much responsibility came with the job title. Plus, Cori's child had experienced trauma when she'd lost her dad. She certainly didn't need any more father figures disappearing from her life.

Of course, that would assume that he was aiming for a serious relationship with a woman he'd met less than six hours ago, which under the current circumstances would more than likely never take place. He needed to be clear on the subject. Especially since every time he spoke to Doctor Cori Parker, his attraction to her kept deepening, almost to the point where he was losing control over his emotions.

He couldn't allow that to happen. Not now. Not when he was busy working on rekindling his relationship with his grandfather. A relationship that seemed to take a negative turn with each hour they were together.

Everything about his grandfather was a mystery to Gage, and that mystery was only part of the puzzle. Gage felt as if he'd somehow stepped out of his entire family for the past ten years and they'd all gone off on different paths and now he was frantically playing catch-up.

Not only had his marriage dissolved in part because of his drinking, but his relationship with his parents, who lived only blocks from him in New York City, had become strained. His sister barely spoke to him after he'd repeatedly showed up at her apartment in the middle of the night wanting to crash on her sofa, and his best friend had told him flat out to stay away after Gage had made a pass at his girlfriend—an accusation Gage denied, but in fact he simply couldn't remember.

He hadn't thought his life could get worse until his divorce became official, and soon after he'd been overlooked for a promotion he thought he'd had. Normally, the combination of the two would have sent him on a long self-indulgent alcohol binge, but somewhere along the line, he'd realized that alcohol only prolonged the misery.

Going sober had been, and continued to be, more difficult than he'd ever imagined. He had decided to do it on his own, with an occasional AA meeting when he was feeling particularly vulnerable. So far it was working. There were still times when all he could think about was a shot of bourbon: the taste of it on his tongue, the heat of it in the back of his throat, the effects of it on his mind and body. There were moments when he'd crave it more than his next breath, but then he'd remind himself of who he'd become because of it and he'd decide all over again that he liked himself much better sober.

And now, his grandfather had demanded he steer clear of the one shining light in all of his post-drinking gloom, Doctor Cori Parker.

Perhaps it was one of those blessings in disguise, and for now, he'd roll with it.

He caught up to his grandfather standing in line at the buffet table, well ahead of May and Hailey. "What's going on, Gramps? Why the cold shoulder for Cori and her grandmother?"

Buck piled potato salad and green beans on his plate. Gage grabbed a plate and opted for the green salad. Most everyone was already seated at the tables and the room echoed their conversations.

"That woman's been persnickety ever since I joined this organization."

"How?"

"I don't want to talk about it now. She'll upset my stomach and I need this here food to keep my blood sugar normal." He turned to Gage. "You'll know why, come the annual auction."

"There's an auction?"

"Yep, and lately they haven't been so good because of that persnickety pill."

Gage grabbed a chicken thigh and leg along with a rack of ribs from the heated pans, piled everything on his plate and then ladled on thick dark-red barbecue sauce from a silver bowl at the end of the table. He couldn't remember the last time he'd eaten barbecue of any kind, especially with an endless supply of sauce. His meals were mostly high-end cuisine in fancy Manhattan restaurants or something organic he'd picked up at a market. This kind of food reminded him of his summers on the ranch in Briggs, Idaho, and he looked forward to chowing down on the memories.

Barbecues on the ranch in Briggs with friends and family were perhaps some of his favorite memories. There were horseshoe games, roping games, potato sack races and long days of endless laughter. Adults and kids would participate. There was never a game that excluded the kids, and there were plenty of kids, cousins mostly, to play with.

What he remembered most clearly about those days, was that even though there was plenty of beer served along with all the barbecue you could eat, no one ever overindulged. No one ever had to be driven home afterward or made a fool of themselves because they were drunk. Everyone seemed to know their limits and stuck to them.

A trait Gage had apparently never learned.

When the day had ended, they sat around a roaring fire singing cowboy songs, telling stories and reciting poems, and Gage had wanted nothing more than to sit out under that starry sky for the rest of his life. On more than one occasion, he'd lean back on the ground, stare up at that dazzling night sky and imagine himself as the hero in one of Zane Grey's books.

"You don't have to worry, Gramps. I can outbid anybody in this room. Just tell me what you want and it's yours."

The thought of buying Grandpa Buck a first-edition Zane Grey novel really appealed to Gage. He loved a good competition. It was in his DNA from playing on Wall Street for the past six years. It was all about the score. All about the win. All about the money. Thanks to his ex-wife, Gage had become addicted to making money, and now that he had made more money than he ever thought possible, it was time to spend some of his cash to help out his family, beginning with Grandpa Buck.

"I don't need your dang money. I can get whatever I want on my own." His voice was stern and somber. Gage didn't understand his reaction. Everyone wanted free money.

"I'm only saying, I can help."

"Don't want it."

"But Gramps, I'm trying to…"

"You try too hard, son. Settle down. I saved us two seats," Buck said. "Make up your mind. Will you be sitting with me or my enemy?"

"With you, of course."

"And no more money talk."

Gage wanted to ask him why, but he let it go. "Whatever you want."

"I want us to enjoy our first meal together in a very long time."

"You got it, Gramps."

"Then our relationship is headed in the right direction."

Grandpa Buck took off for their saved box seats. Gage trailed after him, still wondering what the heck that last blowup was all about. How could his grandfather not accept his generous offer? He'd never experienced such refusal. Before his drinking had taken over his personality, his parents had accepted his money and even asked for a loan when they bought their last apartment. His friends had accepted all the lavish presents he'd given them, and his ex-wife had tried to break him in the final settlement.

Everyone wanted his money except Gramps.

He didn't know how to digest that fact, but he couldn't dwell on it or it would sour his stomach, and right now he wanted nothing more than to dig into those ribs.

As he approached his grandfather's table, he caught Cori's gaze from across the room. Inner passions told him to acknowledge her, but circumstances demanded that he keep focused on the task at hand, pleasing his grandfather. At this point in his overly complicated life, no matter how much he craved Doctor Cori Parker, it was probably better for everyone concerned if he honored his grandfather's wishes and kept his distance… at least for tonight.

Chapter Three

Once the meal had finished, the opening talks welcomed everyone to the yearly conference. There was a video of last year's conference, a couple of letters from members who couldn't make it this year, and a rundown of all the upcoming events, including a train ride up to Silverton, which Hailey was already excited about.

"Are we going on the train ride, Momma? Can we? I've never been on a real train."

"We live in New York City. We're on a train most every day," Cori told her daughter.

"That's a different kind of train. Grammy says this is a real Western train with a real coal-burning engine and everything. I promise not to get a cinder in my eye if we go. Honest."

The speaker had warned them about his getting a cinder in his eye several years ago when he sat in the open railcar.

"I already bought the tickets for us, sweetheart. We're all going," Grandma May said.

"I can't let you pay for us, Gram. That's too much," Cori protested.

Grandma May shook her head. "Nonsense. It's my treat."

The train ride, which was an all-day affair, had been scheduled for Saturday. That was three days away. The conference ended on Sunday with a business meeting and an excursion to Mesa Verde National Park. Cori and her family would be driving back to Gram's house by then, and the conference—along with Gage Remington, given his apparent behavior—would be a fading memory.

All through dinner, Cori had tried to get his attention, but he'd seemed dead-set on avoiding her at all costs. It made Cori believe he took their grandparents' warnings seriously. Although she admired his discipline in the matter, it didn't bode well for them maintaining a friendship, even a clandestine one, which could have been fun.

After all the talks had ended and most of the attendees either went up to their rooms or headed over to the tavern, she walked the somewhat empty sidewalks of downtown Durango in the moonlight, alone. She thought about how nice it would have been to share this with Gage. Whatever was going on between their grandparents certainly shouldn't impact their budding friendship. She wasn't looking for a relationship, at least not with her life so unsettled, but a friendship with a man was something that she'd been missing for a very long time. And Gage Remington seemed like the man for the job. She liked that he seemed to really care about rekindling his relationship with his grandfather, and that he'd taken the time to escort him to Durango. Not very many men would want to do that.

Plus, he had a killer smile.

"Nice night," a familiar voice echoed from behind her. She had heard the rustle of feet on pavement, but never assumed it would be Gage. She felt as if he'd been reading her thoughts, and a tinge of heat made her blush.

His distinctive voice echoed in her ears. "Mind if I join you?"

Cori spun around to see Gage standing close behind her, grinning. At once she noticed how good he looked, with scruffy facial hair, a gray button-down shirt open at the neck, revealing a dusting of dark chest hair, tight black jeans and those sexy black boots. His mere presence made her reconsider those silly friendship thoughts. This cowboy might have to be elevated to a friend with benefits. She'd never thought of that possibility with any other man she'd met, until now.

"Your timing is impeccable. I was just thinking about you." She flipped her hair over her shoulder, and quickly wet her lips.

"In a good way, I hope." His grin grew wider, and his dark eyes sparkled under the glow of the streetlights. Her knees felt weak, and her pulse quickened.

"I thought you were ignoring me."

"I was, and I'm sorry about that. My grandfather is a powerful force, but he finally went up to his room. The good news is I was able to get my own room, so we're both much happier men this evening. And your grandmother?"

"She and Hailey called it a night."

"What about you?"

"I'm in their room. We have a suite."

"No, I mean why aren't you up there with them?"

"I needed a walk. It's too lovely to be inside. Don't you agree?"

"Way too lovely," he said, his gaze caressing her face, a shadow of a smile on his lips. She wanted to swoon, but controlled herself. "Much different from Manhattan."

Cori didn't remember telling him she lived in New York City.

"How'd you know?"

"Know what?"

"Where I'm from?"

"I didn't. That's where I'm from. Been living in New York for the past six years. And you?"

"Wow, it really is a small world... The past five."

They continued up Main Avenue, past closed shops and bustling restaurants. For a few minutes, neither of them spoke, and not a single car passed them on the street. The silence of the town wrapped them in its serenity, as if protecting them from the rest of the hurried world, reminding Cori of her visits to her gram's house when she was a child.

Gage broke the silence as a horse-drawn wagon filled with several tourists went clacking by. "So this is a vacation?"

"Not exactly. More like a major change. I was an ER doctor, but I quit. I'd been working too many hours and not spending any time with Hailey. I needed to slow down and rethink my career path...what's important to me. I don't know exactly where Hailey and I will settle, but I won't be going back to New York. And you? Is this a vacation with your grandfather?"

His soft deep chuckle erupted from the back of his throat, reminding her how much she'd missed the intimate company of a man.

"The words *vacation* and *grandfather* can't be used in the same sentence, at least not where I'm concerned. It's more of an attempt at rekindling some burning embers with my family. I thought I'd start with my grand-father and work forward."

"Sounds as if you burned a lot of bridges."

"More like I soaked them in gasoline and used a flamethrower." His voice took on a serious tone, as if he hadn't liked where his life was heading and now he was seriously trying to change.

"I'm getting a little worried."

"About what?"

"About us."

"Things are looking up. I didn't know we were an *us*."

She chuckled and slowed her pace, wanting to make her intentions clear.

"That all depends."

"On what?"

"On if your arson days are over." She didn't want to begin anything with Gage if he was already focused on the endgame. What few men she had dated in the five years since her husband's passing had only been interested in hookups or sex without any commitment. In the beginning that was fine, but after you've experienced real love, hooking up with men who don't care about you gets old really fast. She wanted something more now, and until she found it, she was willing to stay celibate. At least, that was the plan.

"I'm more into building bridges now. Not that I'm a very good carpenter, but I'm learning."

She nodded, wanting to know more, but willing to wait for the details when and if he was ready to share.

"One plank at a time."

"That's a tough concept for a New Yorker. Especially in my line of work."

"What do you do?"

"I'm a trader."

"A Wall Street trader?"

"Yes, but I'm on an extended leave at the moment."

When she glanced at him, she saw the anxiety on his face. She'd met several traders, both in her practice and socially. If they couldn't be in the center of the action they had a difficult time functioning in general society. They needed that constant tension in order to remain somewhat calm.

"And I take it that's not a state you're comfortable with."

"I'm trying to settle into it, but I have to admit it's more difficult than I'd ever imagined."

"I have a feeling you miss the high-speed pace of the trading floor."

When they came to a corner, they each looked both ways on the deserted streets, and casually made their way across... A far cry from the streets of Manhattan where the traffic never stopped, 24/7.

"There's more to it than the pace. I grew used to getting whatever I wanted, whenever I wanted it. And I grew used to expecting it. More than I'd like to admit. Second row seats at a Knicks game, same-night reservations at any high-end restaurant in Manhattan, first-row theater tickets, whatever. It's hard to explain. I felt as if I was someone important, and that I deserved all that stuff."

"So you were addicted to the power that kind of position brings."

"You sound like my shrink."

"I treated a patient with wealth addiction in 2008 when the stock market crashed. He would have tried to hang himself, because he'd lost several million dollars in three days, but he couldn't find the appropriate Armani belt. At least that's what he told me. He was also a perfectionist, which ultimately saved his life."

He snickered and shook his head. "Are you serious?"

"Absolutely."

"It wasn't like that for me. Usually I was too drunk back then to really care."

Cori abruptly stopped walking. Her heart raced and her stomach was clenched. His words were like a stinging slap. She turned to face him. "What do you mean?"

"Ironic that we should stop walking here in front of Wine and Fine Spirits, a store I would have immediately been drawn to if this were a few months ago."

Cori took stock of her surroundings, and sure enough, just a couple steps up ahead, next to a real estate office, stood a softly lit shop with an inviting open doorway. She walked up to the window and peered inside. High-end wine and spirits crowded the shop. Some of which she would like to buy and bring back to Gram's. Cori loved a smooth Pinot Noir and she spotted a great bottle for only sixty-five dollars.

A steal.

She was thinking how she'd buy a couple of bottles before they left town when Gage said, "I'm a recovering alcoholic. At least that's the term I'm supposed to use. I crave a drink twenty-four-seven, but somehow I manage to control the craving by telling myself I'm better off without it."

"And do you believe you are?"

He moved to get closer to her and stared into her eyes. She saw the vulnerability of a man in need of affection, in need of family, of friends, of a lover...of a drink.

"Moments like this, being this close to you, I would have to say yes. I believe I am."

He gently ran his fingers down the side of her face, like feathers caressing her cheek. She'd so missed a man's touch, his laughter, the intimacy of his affections.

Gage leaned in to kiss her, but at the very last moment she stepped away from him. Reality took hold, stark hurtful reality of a past event that had changed her life forever. She suddenly felt sick to her stomach. Only seconds ago, she'd been daydreaming of his kiss, and now his touch clenched her insides. The mere thought of her being intimate with a recovering alcoholic made her feel as if she was betraying her past and jeopardizing Hailey's future. She envisioned herself running toward a cliff without the ability to stop.

"I'm sorry, but I can't...I can't do this. I need to get over to the hotel. My daughter won't sleep without me tucking her in."

His forehead furrowed, breaking the trance. "Sure. I understand. We can hustle back."

She took a few steps backward, feeling as if being near him was wrong.

"No. That's okay. You continue with your walk. I don't want to force you to come back with me. It's a nice night. You should enjoy it."

He stepped toward her, just as she turned and headed up the sidewalk. She needed to get out of there. Needed to get away from him before she did something she'd regret.

"You're not forcing me to do anything. I want to escort you back to the hotel," he said from behind her.

He caught up to her and tried to take her hand. She snapped it away, as if he was a stranger.

"You're not understanding. I don't want you to come with me. Please. Just let me go. Our grandparents were right. We can't talk to each other anymore."

He stopped walking as she moved ahead of him, leaving him standing on the corner. She jogged across the deserted street, heading straight toward the hotel. She heard him call after her, but she kept moving forward, kept jogging until she stood in front of the hotel, struggling to catch her breath, thinking about what had nearly happened.

How could she have flirted with an alcoholic? Fallen for his charm? It wasn't like her to be taken in so easily. She should have caught the warning signs from the start. His ordering a soda in the bar when they first met should have tipped her off.

As she ran up the three cement steps right outside the lobby, she decided she wanted nothing to do with Gage Remington, no matter what her libido told her. She could not and would not fall for an alcoholic, not when it was a drunk driver who had taken her husband's life.

AFTER A RESTLESS night's sleep, speculating on why Cori had left him standing on the street corner when they'd been having such a nice evening, he awoke thinking he should have simply listened to his gramps. She obviously wasn't interested in any kind of relationship. Or perhaps her grandmother had gotten to her? Or she secretly never liked him and when he pushed it, her true feelings came out? But did she have to run away? He'd never experienced a woman actually running from one of his advances. What was that all about?

All he could conclude from her odd behavior was that she wanted no part of any kind of romantic interlude. That was now crystal clear. He'd just have to learn to suck it up, like his gramps had taught him when he was a kid.

He took in a deep breath and let it out. "I can handle this."

Still, he was hopeful she'd come around.

And maybe it would happen as soon as today. He wasn't exactly ready for a day of horseback riding. The working dude ranch was located just outside of town. Unfortunately, Gramps wouldn't hear of him not participating. Grandpa Buck always loved to ride, no matter if it was on his own ranch wrangling steer or for fun with his friends and family. He'd taught Gage how to ride the summer he'd turned five. It took a while for Gage to get the hang of it, but once he did, his mother had a hard time getting him to do anything else during their visits.

Now, that seemed like light-years ago. He hadn't been on a horse in more years than he cared to remember, and had probably lost his ability to ride. He'd forced himself to not care about ranch life and riding once he began making it on Wall Street. None of that mattered as long as he was moving up the ladder and making an insane amount of money. How could he possibly want to be a cowboy when all of Manhattan was laid out at his feet?

He snickered at the irony of it all.

It seemed this simple trip with his grandfather would be taking him back to something he'd shoved so far back in his mind that riding a horse now seemed foreign to him, almost as though that had been some other kid riding around his grandpa's ranch.

Gramps used to tell him, "You're a natural cowboy, son. And one day, this here ranch will be all yours."

Gage wondered if his grandfather still felt that way, and if he did, what the heck would Gage do with an entire ranch?

Sell it, came rushing into his thoughts. *Take the money and run.*

He took a deep breath as he pulled his car onto the gravel road that led to S & J Ranch. He felt certain he was headed for a day of pure misery.

"We're starting off with a mighty fine breakfast, served outdoors like it should be," Gramps said as Gage drove their car into a spot. "Got my appetite all riled up for some flapjacks, eggs and biscuits this morning."

"Should you be eating flapjacks with your sugar problem?"

Gramps glared at Gage. "What I eat ain't none of your concern. I won't be collapsing again anytime soon, so you don't have to worry. Just stay out of my business and we'll get along fine."

Gage turned off the engine. "I was just trying to…"

"Look, son, I know you're trying to say and do the right things so you and me can get our relationship back on track. There's been a lot of bad blood between us, and it's going to take some time for me to believe you've changed your haughty ways. So please do us both a favor and try not to tell this old cowboy what to do. It brings out my worst side, and right now, being here with all my friends, talking about my favorite writer, I don't need a mother. What I need is my grandson. When you find him let me know, 'cause I miss that rascal more than I wanna say."

Before Gage could respond, his grandfather slipped out of the sedan and walked off toward his friends who were gathering in front of the massive red stables. Everyone shared a smile and a nod as they moved on toward the Old West town that was part of the ranch. Breakfast would be served behind the hotel.

Gage sat there trying to digest what his grandpa had told him. It was the Gramps of his youth who had just lectured him, not the Gramps he'd been traveling with for the past couple of days. That Gramps hadn't spoken a kind word to him since he'd said hello, and even hello had seemed forced.

The good thing was his grandfather had actually spoken to him in a calm voice. Now all Gage had to do to keep the momentum going was find his way back to being "that rascal," so he and his grandfather could rekindle a relationship they both seemed to want more than either one of them was willing to admit.

As he stepped from the car and beeped it locked, another car pulled up, containing Cori, her grandmother and Hailey. Maybe now he could get to the bottom of Cori's speedy departure last night.

"Hey," Hailey said as she bounced out of the car, her white cowgirl hat momentarily slipping from her head, revealing golden curls catching sunlight. Gage could tell she was excited about her day. Her face and demeanor announced it loud and clear.

"All set for the ride?" he asked, eager to engage someone in Cori's family in a conversation.

"You bet. I've never been on a real live horse before,

just the fake kind on a carousel. Have you ever ridden a real horse?"

"Yep, when I was a kid."

"I bet that was a long time ago."

Gage chuckled. Did he look that old? Was thirty-two getting up there? He supposed that to Hailey anyone taller than her had to be old. "It sure was, and I'm a little scared I forgot how."

She shook her head. "You can't forget something like that, silly. It would be like forgetting how to dance. Just because you haven't done it in a long time doesn't mean you forgot how."

"How can you be so sure?"

"Because my dad taught me how to ride a two-wheeler bike when I was three, and after he died and we moved to New York, I had to give my bike away. So I didn't ride in a really long time. Then when we went to visit Grammy, she let me ride her bike and I remembered everything. Even how to use the bell and keep pedaling when someone is in front of me."

Gage wanted to hug her, but he restrained himself. He wondered if all kids were as precocious as Hailey, or was she one of a kind?

"Thank you for telling me that story. I feel much better about riding now."

"You're welcome," she said, beaming.

"I hope Hailey wasn't bothering you," Cori asked once Hailey skipped off with her grandmother, who never really looked his way. Apparently her dislike for Buck Remington was, by default, passed on to his grandson.

"Not at all. She's surprisingly smart. Are all kids her age that smart?"

"I get the feeling you haven't been around children much."

"Hardly ever."

"Most kids are pretty smart these days, but Hailey happens to be more intuitive than other children."

"She takes after her mom," Gage told her, hoping that would help cut through the icy chill.

Regrettably, it didn't, and she began to walk away.

"About last night," he called after her.

She stopped, and spun around to ace him, the sun dancing on her raven hair. She looked absolutely stunning in the morning light wearing a red T-shirt, tight jeans and boots. Gage wanted nothing more than to hold her in his arms and kiss those adorable lips. He knew he shouldn't be feeling this way, knew he needed to take a step back, but the attraction was too strong. And given the way the light embraced her slim body, his thoughts were all about the bedroom, and definitely not about getting up on a horse.

"I told you, I'm honoring my grandmother's wishes, and if you want a relationship with your grandfather, you'll do the same."

Then she abruptly spun on her tan boot heels and left him standing there, exactly as she had the previous night.

"But we don't even know why they're fighting," he yelled after her.

She didn't look back.

CORI HADN'T BEEN horseback riding in years. The last time had to be when she was about twelve or thirteen, she couldn't be sure. Now that she was almost thirty-one, that made it seventeen or eighteen years ago. Way too long. Most likely it had been the last summer she and her mom had gone from their home in Brookhaven, New York, to visit her grandparents. Her dad was a physician with Brookhaven Memorial and seemed to work 24/7. When Cori announced that she was following in his footsteps, her parents did everything to accommodate that goal, including keeping her in school almost year-round.

Cori had been under the misconception that if she could be a doctor like her dad, they'd spend more time together. That never happened. Medical school only gave them less time to spend with each other.

She had so little free time, in fact, that her grandparents started coming out east to visit her and her parents. When Cori was a teenager, summers were dedicated to more school. Her total focus had changed. All her free time was spent studying so she could get into an Ivy League school. Nothing else mattered.

Gone were those long summer days of reading Zane Grey books, wading in the nearest river, baking with Gram, working in the garden with Gramps or flying high on the wooden swing her grandfather had made just for her. He'd hung it from a sturdy branch out in the backyard from a huge oak tree that shaded the entire property.

She didn't resent her parents for helping her achieve her educational goals. Nor did she resent her father for spending most of his time working, which he still did. She only wished they had set aside some time for play in that schedule for success, a pastime Cori would have liked to participate in during her high school years.

Those summers with her grandparents were some of the best memories of her life, and now, watching her daughter's excitement as she saddled up for her first ride on a horse, she realized how much she wanted to re-create those times for her. The difference between herself and her dad was that she needed to be a part of Hailey's life, especially now that Hailey's dad had passed away. She didn't know exactly where they would end up living, or what their life would look like on a daily basis, but whatever she chose for them, it most certainly would not include a man who was an alcoholic, recovering or otherwise.

"Come on, Mom. We're waiting for you," Hailey yelled from a few feet away. She rode a beautiful paint that looked as tame as a bunny rabbit, a trait Cori had insisted on. No way would she allow her daughter to ride anything less. Hailey wore a hard hat, her new Western boots, thick jeans and a pink T-shirt. If Cori could have made her wear body armor, she might have felt a little less frightened about her daughter's first ride.

Of course, she didn't let Hailey see her fear. Cori tried to raise a strong daughter who knew her limits, knew when it was too dangerous and knew when to proceed. Hailey didn't always live up to those expectations, as was evident from her abysmal grades last year in school. And by the growing lack of confidence those falling grades had caused. She and Hailey had had long talks about her schoolwork, with some heavy restrictions attached to those talks. By the end of the school year Hailey had managed to bring up some of those grades, but her self-confidence was still lacking. Cory hoped this move, and spending time with both her and her grammy, would help.

So far, it seemed to be working. However, on this particular morning Cori wasn't so sure whether horseback riding at nine years of age constituted bravery or just plain stupidity. That went for Cori's own apprehensions about getting up on a horse as well.

Fortunately Hailey's horse was pretty small compared to the others, which eased some of her stress. Not so much for her own horse. Her stallion seemed to be taller than the rest—or was that simply her fear talking? She wasn't exactly sure of anything as she tried to stifle her trembling insides.

The Zane Grey conference attendees who thought themselves hardy enough to ride a horse had downed their cookhouse breakfast, received basic pointers on handling their horse and were now waiting for the first group to take off on the designated trail. Their leader, a middle-aged cowboy who sported a handlebar mustache, a trail hat and red scarf, brown fringed chaps over dark blue jeans, a charcoal colored shirt and well-worn Western boots had a disposition that even the sternest cowboy would have admired.

Standing next to Tonto, a honey-colored stallion, Cori figured she'd hesitated long enough. The wrangler, an older teenager with handsome rugged looks that probably drove the local teen girls to delirium, stood by, holding on to Tonto and patiently waiting for her to mount. It was time. She couldn't put it off any longer. She took a deep breath, and mumbled a request as she grabbed the reins. "Please be good to me, Tonto, and I'll try to remember everything I learned about riding."

Tonto held steady as she slipped her foot into the stirrup, grabbed the horn on the saddle and in one smooth movement lifted her body up onto the horse. She gently rested her bottom in the saddle. Tonto took a step to regain his footing and in what seemed like an instant, Cori felt as comfortable as she always had whenever she was on horseback. All her fears and apprehensions vanished as soon as she guided Tonto in the right direction.

"You good?" the young wrangler asked as he took a step back from the horse.

"Perfect," Cori answered, the smile on her face so big her cheeks hurt.

Her grandmother and Buck were up ahead in the advanced group. Of course, they both kept their distance from each other. Gram had planted herself near the beginning of the line, while Buck was second to last.

Once Cori joined the beginners group, she spotted Gage at the back of her line. She assumed that, just like her, he hadn't had much opportunity to ride while living in New York City. Or perhaps she was completely wrong about him, and he could ride with the best of them but had stayed behind in order to persuade her to warm up to him again. He was wasting his time. It would take nothing short of a miracle for her to ever let her guard down.

Hailey was directly behind her, which made her a bit uncomfortable. However, it was the spot that Hailey had chosen, so Cori forced herself to go along with it.

As soon as everyone had mounted, the lead cowboy started up the trail. Cori's horse seemed to know what to do with merely the slightest nudge, which made the ride much more pleasurable. It didn't take long before Cori relaxed and allowed herself to enjoy the trip through some of the most beautiful country she'd seen in years. Whenever she glanced back at Hailey, a wide grin seemed glued to her little face.

The trail wound down a forested hillside with a view of a river where some guests were busy panning for gold while others cast their fishing lines in the lazy water. It was truly a beautiful day, and with each movement of her horse, Cori's appreciation of the moment grew by leaps and bounds, especially knowing that Hailey was enjoying it as much as she was.

"Don't panic," the teen wrangler yelled from behind her. "Hold on to the reins and keep your balance!"

Cori heard the thunder of hooves hitting ground before she could see them. Then in a flash of color she saw her daughter whiz by on her runaway horse, leaning forward, holding on for dear life. The horse kicked out its back legs but kept going. Before the group leader could get his bearings, Gage took off after Hailey with the group leader right behind him. She could see Hailey leaning off to the side, looking as if she was going to topple over. In the next instant, Gage had reached out and guided her back up on her saddle, motioning for her to hold on to the horn with both hands. She must have done as she was told, because she was able to right herself and stay on the horse.

Cori's heart clattered against her chest as she took off after her daughter without giving it a single conscious thought. She knew exactly how to get her horse to run and how to position her body for the speed. It seemed almost second nature to her and she realized that all her apprehensions about riding had been a waste of energy. When push came to shove, those childhood riding skills that her grandparents had drummed into her had kicked in. "Hold on, Hailey," she yelled as she rode after her baby.

Then, just as quickly as Hailey's horse had taken off, it stopped. Gage had managed to get in front of it with his chocolate-colored stallion, and when Hailey's paint approached, it slowed to a trot and nuzzled up to Gage's horse as if it knew it had done something wrong.

"Hailey, are you all right. Are you okay?" Cori yelled as she approached.

"Woo-hoo!" Hailey yelled. "Was it supposed to do that? That was really fun."

"No," Gage told her. "We're only supposed to be walking. What the heck happened?"

Hailey seemed breathless. "I don't know, but I think it didn't like the big ugly rat we saw back there on the trail."

"It was probably a possum," the group leader said. "You did everything right, Hailey. You're one brave little girl."

"I only did what you told us to do."

"Are you sure you're all right?" Cori asked as she tried to calm her fears. "I think that's enough riding for one day. Maybe we should return to the barn."

"But I don't want to quit yet. Besides, that mean ol' possum is probably hiding under a bush by now. I like this, Momma. Can we please keep going?"

"I'll ride alongside her," Gage said. "She'll be fine. I promise."

Cori didn't want to cause her daughter to fear riding a horse. It was one of those moments in life when you either kept going or retreated forever. Cori believed in moving forward, and she wanted her daughter to have the same values.

She turned to Gage. "You'll stay right with her?"

"All the way," he said.

The rest of their group of ten had gathered around them, all waiting for Cori's reply. Even Grandma May had backtracked when she'd heard the commotion and was encouraging Cori to say yes. "She's got your spunk, Corina-May. You can't discourage her now."

"Fine, but I'll be right behind you," Cori told her daughter.

A loud whoop went up from the group as Hailey cheered and whistled her excitement. Soon all the horses were back in line behind the leader making their way along the grassy path.

Cori guided her horse up next to Gage. "Thank you," she told, him while thinking a mere thank-you could never be enough. "That was some pretty fancy riding for a New Yorker."

"Hailey was right. You never forget how."

"Sometimes kids know more about these things than adults do." Cori took a deep breath, then let it out. "I'd like to do something to repay you for stopping her horse."

"Not necessary. I didn't do anything special."

"Sure you did. How 'bout if I buy you dinner tonight? I don't think there's much going on this evening for the conference—a light business meeting and a book discussion. We wouldn't be missing anything too important."

"Thanks, but I don't think your grandmother likes me very much."

"After what you did, she probably loves you. But she won't be joining us. She'll be attending the activities at the conference."

"Sure," he said before she could tell him that Hailey would be joining them.

"Five o'clock in the lobby?"

"Perfect," he said, then tipped his hat and smiled over at her. In that instant, Cori knew her determination to stay away from this man was going to be more difficult than she ever thought possible.

ON THE DRIVE BACK to the hotel, Gramps didn't seem to want to let up on what he called Gage's heroism.

"You done good, son. Made me proud to be your grandfather. I knew you had it in you to be a hero. It's just been stifled for a spell. How'd you know what to do to stop that spooked horse? Did I teach you that?"

Gage wasn't sure he liked all this adulation. He'd gotten his fill at the ranch, when not only did all the wranglers want to know where he'd learned to ride like that but the owner came out and congratulated him while he was grooming his horse.

"I really didn't think about it, Gramps. It just happened. And yes, I believe you did teach me to ride in front of a charging horse. I never had use for that technique when I was visiting you, but I guess I tucked it away in my subconscious. If someone had asked me about that move before I did it, I don't think I would've been able to remember anything. Funny how your mind retains certain things and you can conjure them up whenever you need them."

Gage still had a hard time believing that had been him on that horse: that his riding had come so naturally and he hadn't even thought about not going after Hailey. If this had been six months ago, he wouldn't have been able to go after her.

He would have been too drunk.

"And how'd it make you feel savin' that there little girl?"

Without missing a beat, Gage said, "Like a cowboy. Like a real cowboy."

Chapter Four

Cori had tried on every outfit in her suitcase, but none of them seemed appropriate for her dinner date with Gage. She told herself a million times over there was nothing more to this date than thanking him for saving her daughter, and still she'd taken three antacids trying to get her stomach to behave. It wasn't as if they'd be alone in some dark romantic restaurant. Hailey would be there with them. Still, Cori couldn't seem to let go of the nerves.

"You look beautiful, Momma," Hailey told her each and every time she'd modeled a new ensemble for her.

"You're not helping. If I look beautiful in the black outfit and beautiful in the gray outfit, how can I trust your opinion?"

Hailey threw up her arms. "Because you look beautiful in everything!"

Love bubbled up for her sweet daughter. "How about if I wear my pajamas? Or Grammy's robe? How would I look in those?"

Hailey giggled. "Don't be silly, Mom. You know we can't wear pajamas outside. Only babies can wear their pajamas to a restaurant. You need to wear regular clothes."

"And which regular clothes do you like best?"

"I like your black cowgirl boots, your purple swirly skirt and the red blouse you bought in that little store with the white chair I could sit on while you tried on clothes. The store near Grammy's house."

Shopping for a dress or something other than slacks and a shirt had been something Cori rarely did at home. She never had the time. Her closet was filled with casual work clothes and little else. She rarely went out on a date, and even when she did, she had gone right from work and worn her usual black dress pants and a dark-colored blouse. The same clothes were worn when she'd meet a friend for drinks. Not that she had liked going out for drinks with her friends. All they seemed to want to do was fix her up with someone they thought would be "perfect for her." Her friends were well-meaning, but the dates had been disastrous nonetheless. Eventually, she'd stopped accepting drink invitations, and her friends stopped all the matchmaking.

When she quit her job and told her friends she was moving to Colorado they gave her a going-away party. And once again, she'd worn dress slacks and a white blouse.

Truly pathetic.

"But I haven't tried that combination on for you. How do you know I'll look good in it?"

Hailey grinned. "I just know."

"Fine," Cori said as she hurriedly changed into the suggested outfit, thinking purple and red would never look good together. Plus, she didn't want to wear a skirt. She felt more comfortable in pants, and above all, she wanted to feel relaxed.

Just as she tucked in her blouse, she turned back to

her daughter, who'd busied herself with the latest book she'd uploaded to her touch-screen tablet.

"So how does this look?" she asked.

Cori shifted her feet, uncomfortable with the skirt that showed her knees, sure it looked unflattering or that she was trying too hard...the one thing she absolutely did not want Gage to think. After all, this was simply a friendly dinner. Payback for his quick thinking on a horse.

Nothing more.

"Oh, Momma, you look spectacular!" Hailey's face lit up with a great big smile.

"Spectacular, huh?"

Hailey eagerly nodded as Cori walked past her to the full-length mirror hanging on the back of the bathroom door, certain the colors clashed and she'd be changing once again. Instead, as soon as she stood in front of the mirror and gazed at her reflection, she liked what she saw. The blouse and skirt blended together perfectly, as if she'd purchased them as a set. And the boots gave the outfit just the right amount of sassy country flair. It made her feel like a woman, instead of a faceless doctor.

"You're pretty good at this fashion stuff," Cori told her daughter.

Hailey shrugged, deadpan. "Just one of my many talents."

Then she giggled again and Cori couldn't help but giggle with her.

"How did you know these colors would work?" Cori asked as she twisted to see the back of her outfit in the mirror.

"Mom, I know fashion. I read about it all the time.

Why do you think I want to be a fashion designer when I grow up?"

"You do?" As soon as Cori said it she wanted to take it back. How could she not know what her own daughter's aspirations were?

She went over to Hailey and sat on the bed next to her, stroking her silken hair, feeling sick over the fact that her daughter had probably told her about these fashion plans, but Cori had been too distracted by fatigue from her long hours in the ER to focus.

"I'm sorry. I should have known that already. Can you forgive me?"

"Oh, Momma. You couldn't have known, 'cause I never told you before this very minute. I've been thinking about it for a long time. Susan's mom helped me find some schools." Hailey sat up, crossed her legs and brought up some pictures on her tablet. "She said the easiest school for me to get into would be Parsons back in New York." She turned the computer toward her mom, then ran a finger over the screen to bring up the next picture. "But London has a lot of fashion programs and that's where Stella McCartney studied, and I *love* Stella's clothes. Then there's a school in Paris that I can't pronounce, but if I went there, they only speak French, so that's a problem. I haven't made up my mind for sure yet, but doesn't it sound like fun?"

Cori leaned back on the bed, exhausted by just listening to Hailey. "But you're not even ten years old."

"You told me you were eight when you decided you wanted to be a doctor just like Grandpa. I'm already nine!"

Cori reached over to stroke her daughter's hair.

"Sweetheart, I want you to have some fun. To play. To be a kid. To have a pet other than a goldfish."

"I'd like a dog. A great big dog that loves everybody."

"Me, too. That's why we're here with Grammy. I didn't get to have a lot of fun once I decided what I wanted to be. Most of my free time was filled with extra classes and summer school. I'm not saying there's anything wrong with that, but what I am saying is you have time to make those decisions. You don't have to make them now. Give yourself a few more years to decide. Who knows, you may want to be a cowgirl and take up barrel racing or mounted shooting when you grow up."

"Can I go to school for those things in New York City?"

Cori smiled. "I don't think so. You'd have to learn those sports on a working ranch."

"Like the one we were on today?"

"Just like the one we were on today."

Hailey thought for a moment. "Is that why Gage rides so well? Does he live on a ranch?"

"He used to visit his grandpa's ranch when he was your age. I think his grandpa taught him how to ride."

"Do you think Gage or his grandpa would teach me how to ride like that if I asked them?"

A sudden vision swept across Cori's mind of Gage teaching Hailey how to ride, of the three of them riding under a vast blue sky surrounded by lush mountains. "I doubt we'll have enough time in Durango for him to teach you. But I can teach you once we're back at Grammy's. I'm sure there's a ranch somewhere near her house."

Hailey rolled over on her back and stared up at the

ceiling. "Now I don't know what I want to be. I thought I had it all figured out, just like Susan. She knows she wants to be a lawyer exactly like her parents. They even picked out her school. How can I tell her I don't know if I want to be a cowgirl or a fashion designer? She won't want to be my best friend anymore."

Cori sat up. "Would it matter to you if Susan changed her mind and didn't want to go to law school?"

Hailey shook her head. "Not the tiniest bit."

"Then why do you think Susan will feel any different about what you want to do?"

Hailey thought about it for a moment. "Momma, you're the smartest person in the whole world."

And she gave her mom a great big hug. "The whole world's a pretty big place. How about if I'm the smartest person in this hotel room? And even then, I think you might be smarter."

"Nope. Grammy's the smartest 'cause she told me to tell you to wear your red blouse and purple skirt. She said Gage would like it."

"What? So it wasn't because you want to be a fashion designer?"

"Sure I do. Maybe. If I can't be a cowgirl, but the clock says four-forty-five. Aren't we supposed to meet Gage in the lobby now?"

Cori glanced at her watch and sure enough they were running late.

"We sure are. Are you ready?"

"I've been ready for the past hour."

"Well, then, let's go."

Within minutes they were walking out of their room toward the staircase at the end of the short hallway. All Cori could think about as they hurried down the stairs was that vision of the three of them on horseback. She knew that could never happen in a million years. Still, the vision remained as she popped another antacid to help with the constant flutter in her stomach.

"I DON'T REALLY take kindly to your having a date with Doctor Parker, but seeing as how it's only payback for some good riding this morning, I'm gonna let it slide… this time." Buck stood in the small bathroom in front of the vanity mirror and combed his wispy hair to one side with what had to be a horsetail brush. Gage remembered those fat brushes from his many visits to the ranch. He had memories of his grandfather brushing his lush brown hair with that very brush, only now Gramps' hair had turned white and was about as lush as a maple tree in winter.

"Thanks, but this feud you and Cori's grandmother have needs to be resolved."

Gage had walked over to his grandfather's room wanting to get to the bottom of the argument between May and Buck, but so far Buck hadn't been very cooperative.

"Ain't never going to happen, son." He slapped on a few drops of Old Spice aftershave and the scent brought back so many memories Gage had a hard time keeping them organized. The best one happened to be the night Buck was getting ready for his thirty-fifth wedding anniversary dinner with his beloved wife, Rose. The whole family would be attending, along with several neighbors. Grandma Rose had wanted the party at a restaurant in town so she wouldn't end up having to cook or clean up afterward. It took some doing, but Grandpa Buck finally gave in and the entire party of fifty all met at Sammy's Smokehouse on the outskirts of Briggs, Idaho. It was the first time Gramps had allowed Gage to wear some of his aftershave, and he remembered how grownup it had made him feel.

He was twelve at the time.

"Can I wear a little of that, Gramps?"

His grandfather stared at Gage through the mirror. "I thought men like you only wore that fancy stuff that costs more than my boots?"

"Not tonight." Gage held out his hand for the familiar cream-colored bottle.

Buck spun around, and handed him the bottle. "Go easy. This stuff can have a powerful effect on a woman."

Gage chuckled, taking the bottle from his grandfather. "How so?"

"The first time I wore that there aftershave, I met your grandmother at the train station in Boise. I was getting off the train and she was getting on. We should'a passed each other right on by, but this here scent caught her attention."

Gage had heard the story many times before, never knowing that Old Spice had been the catalyst.

"And she said, 'Hello, cowboy.' Am I right?"

"Yep, and I got right back on that there train. I didn't care where it was going, as long as I was going along with her."

Guilt and remorse overpowered Gage. "Gramps, I'm so sorry I didn't come back to the ranch after I learned she was so sick. There's no excuse for my behavior. I only hope you can forgive me."

Buck rested a hand on Gage's shoulder. "Keep doing what you're doing, and we might mend our fences after all. But that requires you staying out of my business, and not trying to get me to like folks who I ain't got no time for and you shouldn't either, if you know what's good for you. And so far, from what I see, you don't know squat about what's good for you, except for maybe them boots. Good quality working boots if I ever saw a pair. Maybe there's hope for you after all." He opened the room door to leave. "That is, if you can keep your bedroom thoughts away from Doctor Parker. If she's anything like her grandmother, they'll be hell to pay for in your future, that's for dang sure."

And he walked out of the room, leaving Gage only more confused about the grandparents' feud. A feud that had to end, or Gage would one day soon have to choose between his grandfather and Doctor Cori Parker. A choice he truly did not want to ever make.

"Don't be scared, Mom," Hailey said as she and Cori descended the stairs to the hotel lobby. "Gage is really nice."

Hailey wore her new cowgirl boots and a floral full-skirt dress. She liked dresses and skirts better than pants, and for the most part her wardrobe reflected an eclectic mix of styles. Cori wondered if her daughter would actually become a fashion designer.

"Who said I was scared?"

Hailey took her mother's hand as they rounded the last step that brought them into the lobby. "You don't have to say it out loud. I can tell."

Cori wanted to correct Hailey's analysis of the situation, but before she could say a word she spotted Gage standing in the center of the bustling lobby. As soon as he saw them, his face beamed with anticipation, reminding Cori once again to keep her emotions in check. This was merely payback for his quick thinking on the horse. Nothing she couldn't have done if she'd had her wits about her when she saw Hailey gallop away.

"You both look lovely," Gage offered as they approached.

"And you look like a cowboy out of one of Grammy's Zane Grey books," Hailey announced, all full of smiles and cheer.

"Is that a good thing, or do I look corny?" Gage asked.

"It's a great thing! Who doesn't like a cowboy?" Hailey explained as she skipped toward the front door.

Gage looked at Cori, obviously seeking her approval. He wore his black Western hat, a black T-shirt that hugged his chest—accentuating every muscle—black jeans that hugged everything else and black boots. Hailey had been right. Cori absolutely liked this cowboy. His fast reaction had saved her daughter from what could have been a terrible fall.

"She has a point," Cori told him. "Not many people dislike cowboys."

"How about you?"

"After what happened this morning, I'd say cowboys are way up there on my approval list."

"Even when they live in New York City?"

"Urban cowboys are the absolute best. Especially when they can ride like you do."

A slow grin spread across his face, creasing his lips and causing his whiskey-colored eyes to reflect his joy. "Then, Ma'am, let me escort you to our destination?"

She worked hard at not letting her feelings for him get the better of her, knowing perfectly well she could never fall for a man who struggled with alcohol. Despite the flutter in her stomach, she felt certain this date was merely platonic.

Nothing more…until he took her hand and guided her out the front doors and the scent of Old Spice wafted in the air, a scent that reminded her of long summer days on her grandparents' ranch. A scent that made her feel warm and safe, a scent she hadn't thought about in years. Her grandfather had worn Old Spice and she had worshiped him. He had been an inspiration to her for her entire childhood and when he passed, all those memories he liked to share with her had passed with him. Her grandfather was a true cowboy and had worked on ranches all over the West from the time he was fifteen years old. He met her gram on a ranch in Texas, when he was in his late twenties and she was barely nineteen. She'd come from Chicago and worked as a cook in the main house. They courted for a few months, then were married and moved out to Colorado, where they settled.

They never owned a ranch of their own, but her grandpa always managed to get work to support his family. He encouraged self-confidence and self-reliance. He was a kind and gentle man, who taught Cori she could be and do whatever she set her mind to. It was a belief that had guided her through most of the major decisions of her life, a belief that had guided her to quit her job and move out west, confident that she could make a better life for herself and her daughter. Confident that she didn't need anyone's help. Now, as Gage held her hand and the familiar scent surrounded her and she felt the strength and comfort of his touch, she wasn't sure about anything.

BEFORE DINNER, HAILEY wanted to visit the Train Museum near The Palace Restaurant just off Main Street. Cori had told him she'd made a reservation at the restaurant for five o'clock—a crazy hour to eat dinner. Gage never ate before eight, but this was Durango. He had to go with the flow.

"So you like trains? Does that go for subways, as well? Because you strike me more as a cab kind of guy," Cori said as she and Gage followed Hailey up the sidewalk.

They headed toward the museum, which seemed to be located next to the railroad tracks, past the gift shop—at least that was the direction Hailey was headed in.

"And what does a cab person look like, exactly?"

"Rushed. Scheduled. Not one who deviates from their plans."

Once again, Doctor Cori Parker instinctively knew how he operated. He didn't know how she knew more about what made him tick than anyone else, but he liked it, liked how she got him. Now all he had to do was figure out what she was all about. How difficult could that be?

She made him smile and he felt all warm on the inside. "And here I thought I was well on my way to becoming more spontaneous."

"The train museum is a good start."

He took her hand in his. "Well, then, what are we waiting for?" And they ran to catch up with Hailey, who was already inside.

Gage paid their entrance fee, and soon they were surrounded by everything train. From detailed model trains running through miniature towns, past drive-ins and along hillsides, to full-size locomotives and private cars decked out with Victorian opulence, ready to be occupied by the wealthy owners of their day. From the second Gage stepped into the museum, the tension of the day and perhaps the entire year slipped away from him. Thanks to a kid's curiosity, he'd been forced to slow down, to enjoy the moment, to be in the present without thinking about the future. He found himself meandering through each room, losing all sense of time, reading each description and story, fascinated by everything he saw, touched and read. He felt like a sponge absorbing all that surrounded him, as if the wonder of his youth had taken over and successfully pushed out the obsessive addict he had become.

When he spotted the model depicting the 1950s operation of the Denver & Rio Grande Western railroad complete with the train passing a miniature drive-in theater, it brought back vivid memories.

"There was a Spud Drive-In in Briggs, Idaho, that my grandparents would take me to at least a couple times during each visit," Gage told Hailey as they stood side-by-side in front of the large reproduction. A night at Spud Drive-In was one of the highlights of his trips. There was nothing like watching a movie from the back of a pickup truck.

"What's a drive-in?" Hailey asked.

"You don't know?"

Hailey shook her head.

"All the drive-ins have closed in my grandmother's town. I never got the chance to take her," Cori explained.

Gage leaned in closer to the reproduction, pointing to the tiny drive-in and all the cars lined up in front of the screen. Hailey leaned in closer as well, their heads almost touching. Gage pointed out the tiny concession stand behind all the cars, complete with tiny families walking in and out of the open doors.

"Let me see if I can explain it. A drive-in was more than just a place where you could watch a movie outdoors, it was a place where you could watch that movie while you glanced up at all the stars in the sky. Where you could wear your PJs and snuggle up with a pillow in the back of a pickup truck. You could bring a bucket of popcorn that you'd made at home, and soda in a cooler and whatever else you wanted to bring. You could talk if you wanted to, and no one would complain because they were way over there in their own car or truck." He pointed to the miniature cars in front of the screen.

"That sounds like fun," Hailey said. "You aren't allowed to talk in a movie theater."

"I know, and sometimes you just have to comment on what you're seeing up on the screen. Right?"

She nodded.

"Well, at a drive-in, you can."

"I think I'd like that. My daddy and me watched a movie outside once on his laptop. We were waiting for my mom to get off work so we could all go ice-skating in the park. We watched *Finding Nemo* while we sat on a bench and waited. We didn't have any popcorn or anything to drink, but I got to cuddle with my daddy while we waited and he didn't mind if I talked during the movie 'cause there wasn't anybody around to hear us. I think I'd really like a drive-in, and I bet my daddy would've liked one, too."

Gage couldn't help but give her a little hug.

"I'm sure he would have, very much," Gage said in a low voice as emotion swept over him.

"You know what?" Cori asked, her voice cracking before she cleared her throat.

"What?" Hailey asked as she walked over to her mom and took her hand.

"We've been in here for more than two hours. Are either of you getting hungry yet?"

"I think I've been hungry for the past decade," Gage said, feeling emotionally drained.

"I wasn't trying to be philosophical. I'm merely asking about dinner."

He smiled at her sense of humor.

"Y'know, I've lived in New York City for almost ten years and not once have I stepped into any of the museums or art galleries. How about you? I bet you know them all."

"I've been inside most of them, but only because I thought Hailey needed the experience. If you asked me what I saw, I know more about this museum than anything I've been to in New York. It's nice to have the time to meander through this place. Thanks for agreeing to postpone dinner so we could do this."

"No problem, but we should be thanking Hailey."

"You're welcome. I knew you guys would like it here," Hailey said as she reached for Gage's hand and walked between them toward the exit sign.

They made their way out of the museum and headed toward the restaurant still holding hands, acting like a tight little family. Gage remembered walking between his parents and, on occasion, between his grandparents, holding hands, tugging on them to walk faster or to skip with him. He thought about how safe he'd felt and how much he loved each of them.

He wasn't quite sure he understood his emotions now. He'd been drowning out his feelings with booze for so long he didn't quite know what to make of the wave of affection he felt for both Cori and her daughter.

He'd started drinking in college, to celebrate a good grade on a test, or just because it was fun to get drunk with friends. After graduation he'd find excuses to have a few drinks during happy hour with his contemporaries. Once he was married, and the pressure to make more and more money started, he'd linger with his friends at a bar after work so he wouldn't have to go home and listen to another lecture on how he wasn't trying hard enough to succeed and get ahead.

After a while, he crossed some sort of threshold where he'd have a drink before he went in to work, during lunch, during a break or simply whenever he could sneak one in.

He learned how to control his intake most of the time. His binges were rare, but when he had one, he couldn't remember much, and had to rely on whoever was with him to relay the details of what had happened. And even then he rarely believed what they had to say.

Then, about six months ago, for no other reason than he wanted to see what it would feel like to go through an entire day without a buzz, he stopped drinking and hadn't had one since.

What he was experiencing for Cori was something else entirely, and he had a problem pinpointing the exact emotion. He didn't know where this budding relationship would lead, but for now, with everything else he had going on in his life, it was enough that he was enjoying her company.

ON THE WAY back to the hotel, after a delicious meal of local prime rib with all the trimmings and conversations about what they'd seen at the train museum and museums in New York City, Cori was in no hurry to get back to her room. The weather was balmy, the moon was full, and Cori wanted to spend a little more time getting to know Gage Remington.

Hailey had spotted her Grammy up ahead, walking along the sidewalk with two other women from the conference, and had dashed off to be with her. That left Cori and Gage alone, a situation Cori had hoped to avoid but now welcomed. The entire evening had been surprisingly delightful, and despite Cori's earlier apprehensions, she found herself drawn to Gage more than she'd like to admit.

"She's a great kid," Gage said as Hailey ran up ahead. The hotel was only a couple blocks away, but it seemed to take forever for them to reach it.

"Thanks, I think so, too."

"Nice night," Gage finally said after a couple of awkward minutes.

"Beautiful," Cori agreed.

"Well, now that we've established the good weather, what else do you want to talk about?"

Cori chuckled.

"Was that the real name of your drive-in? Spud?"

"It's Idaho. What can I say? Home of the russet potato. There's even a Miss Russet pageant, just in case Hailey is ever interested in competing. Of course, I'm fairly sure she has to be a resident of Idaho and at least sixteen years old. So there's plenty of time. You might consider putting down roots in Idaho so she doesn't miss out."

He really was very charming. "And where will you be putting down roots?"

"I live in New York City, remember?"

Her forehead furrowed. She knew there would be little chance he could stay off booze if he went back to his job and that city. "Oh, that's right. You're a recovering alcoholic with the high-stress profession that affords you high-end entertainment. How long do you think you'll last back there?"

He stopped walking. "You like coming to the point of the matter, don't you?"

"I'm an ER doctor. I've learned that getting to the truth saves lives."

He hesitated as a horse-drawn wagon went by. When it passed, he said, "Truthfully? I don't know where else to go where I'd fit in."

"Gosh, I don't know. You seemed to fit right in up on that horse today."

"I didn't do anything that any of those other cowboys couldn't have done."

"You just referred to yourself as a cowboy."

"No, I didn't. What I said was… I did, didn't I?"

"It's rubbing off."

"What is?"

"Durango. Zane Grey. The cowboy mystique. Before you know it, you'll be giving rides to tourists just like that cowboy." She nodded in the direction of the cowboy standing in front of the horse-drawn covered wagon that had just passed them.

"Well, then, let's try it on for size." He held out his hand to her as if to assist her into the wagon.

"Oh, no thanks," Cori immediately told him. She wanted to get back up to her room. Spending time alone with Gage was proving to be much too easy, and she wasn't sure it was a smart move for either of them.

"Why not? It looks like fun, and I'm working on my inner cowboy, remember? This is exactly what the doctor ordered, correct?"

"I, um, Hailey would love this." Cori absolutely did not want to get into that wagon without her daughter. She looked up the street for Hailey, and just as she did, her phone beeped, signaling a text message. Reaching into her purse, she pulled out her phone and read:

I have Hailey. We're off to find ice cream. Enjoy your evening!

"I don't see her up ahead," Gage said. "I think she and your gram already went back to their room."

"Actually, they went in search of ice cream."

"Then it's just you and me, kid."

He reached for Cori's hand and waited as she hesitated for a few seconds, nodding his head in the direction of the wagon.

The cowboy climbed up front on his seat, as if she'd already made up her mind, which she most certainly had not.

"C'mon. It'll be fun. We have the whole wagon to ourselves."

That was the problem, she thought, but she couldn't say it out loud.

"Come on. Consider this the Western version of a ride through Central Park."

"I've never been."

"Me neither. So isn't it about time we did?"

"Durango is hardly Central Park."

"And we'd like to keep it that way," the cowboy offered.

Gage beckoned her with one hand, and with the other grabbed hold of the back of the wagon, getting ready to pull himself up onto the small step.

One of the two horses whinnied, and scrapped its hoof on the tarmac.

"Dark Ryder agrees with me," the cowboy said, chuckling. He wore traditional cowboy clothing, including brown chaps and a dark brown Western hat, but there was something about him that caused Cori to believe he was new to the world of cowboying, maybe it was his hat. It didn't quite fit him properly and he kept readjusting it on his head.

She knew focusing on the cowboy was merely avoiding the real issue, so she took a deep breath and zoned in on Gage instead. That smile of his sent her heart racing, and those whiskey-colored eyes melted her insides. His kindness toward Hailey only made her like being with him more than she should. Gage simply sent her into an emotional tailspin, and despite her best efforts she couldn't seem to pull out of her certain demise.

With cautious acceptance, she took his hand in hers and immediately felt the warmth of his touch spread over her entire body. He helped her climb up into the back of the large wagon that could easily hold eight people, convinced that by the end of the ride through town, her resolve to keep her distance from Gage Remington would be completely shattered.

The man was entirely too charming for her own good.

Chapter Five

No doubt about it, Gage Remington was now on the right track with both his grandfather and Doctor Cori Parker. No matter how badly he had wanted to kiss her and whisk her away to his private room last night, he had acted like the perfect gentleman. His psychologist would be proud of his self-control, a trait he'd all but abandoned. So now, as he settled onto a chair next to his grandfather inside the Henry Strater Theater, waiting for the annual auction to begin, he felt good about himself.

It had already been a long morning, but due to his newfound ability to restrain himself, he'd cultivated a new tolerance to his grandfather's dissatisfaction with just about everything. Grandpa Buck hadn't liked most items in the buffet breakfast line that morning, and instead had ordered a Denver omelet with added jalapeño peppers. His coffee hadn't been strong enough, and his orange juice hadn't been fresh enough. Gage figured that Gramps was simply missing the way his wife would dote on him, and let it go at that.

Gage, in contrast, had enjoyed his breakfast, including the mellow coffee and the tart cranberry juice.

Grandpa Buck had lingered over the silent auction memorabilia in the other room, deciding what he wanted to bid on as if each item had some special significance. In the end, he'd hardly bid on anything, despite Gage having encouraged him to bid on just about everything.

"Keeping my money for the auction itself," Buck had told him. "I heard the Keelson's donated some of Zane's fishing poles, and I intend to get me one. That is, if that persnickety pill, May Meriwether, don't outbid me."

"Don't worry about it, Gramps. I can afford to buy you anything you want."

Gramps hadn't responded to the offer until they had found seats and even the seats were cause for debate.

"I don't need your money," Gramps told Gage in no uncertain terms as he settled into the end chair. "I saved up for this event all year, and there ain't no way I'm gonna let you waltz in here and make all that scrimpin' a waste of my time."

"You can keep your money for something you really want to do," Gage countered, as he made himself comfortable in the chair next to his grandfather and next to a chair with a black purse that looked familiar to Gage.

"I'm already doing what I want. I don't need you to interfere."

"Fine," Gage told him, trying desperately not to get exasperated. "But if you change your mind, let me know."

"I won't," Gramps stated, defiantly.

The room buzzed with anticipation. Even Gage felt the excitement of the moment. He had loved Zane Grey's books when he was a kid, *Riders of the Purple Sage*, in particular, and still admired the determination and the adventurous spirit of the author. Zane, like Gage's grandfather when he was a very young man, had traversed the globe when traveling was accomplished only by sheer determination of the individual. They'd both done big-game fishing in oceans, streams and seas that were crowded with fish double and sometimes triple their size. Zane had helped develop his own reel and poles that could snare those kinds of goliaths with little effort.

His grandfather had saved his money from putting in long hours working on ranches throughout the West, and little by little he cobbled together a spread in eastern Idaho that rivaled any other ranch in the Teton Valley. Despite countless setbacks both financial and personal—the accidental death of his older brother being one of them—by the time he was thirty-five, he not only ran a lucrative cattle ranch, but he produced more russet potatoes than any other farmer in the area.

Both men were a testament to the American spirit, to the American cowboy and to what the West and the miles of open land had meant to them.

Emotions welled up inside of Gage as he sat next to his grandfather, a man who represented everything Zane Grey had written about: the true American cowboy.

Three women sat at a folding table off to the right of the stage. Each of them played a role in keeping tabs on the details of the auction. Numbered paddles had been handed out to the eager participants. Numerous cardboard boxes were stacked up on the stage, along with movie posters in various sizes. Hailey and two other older boys stood at the ready to deliver the memorabilia to the winning bidder, while the president of the Zane Grey West Society gave the opening statement.

As the president told the impatient group about some

of the items that would be coming up for auction and how the event would be handled, Gage spotted Cori and her grandmother entering the room. His heart slammed against his chest just watching Cori walk toward him. Fortunately, his gramps didn't see them come in. He was too busy concentrating on the speaker.

Then, in what had to be a turn of fate, the two women took their seats, which happened to be at Gage's table.

"What the heck, son?" Grandpa Buck whispered.

Gage held up his hands in surrender. "I had no idea."

"Did you plan this?" Grandma May asked Cori.

"No. Of course not."

"Is there a problem?" the speaker asked staring right at him and the group at his table, everyone in the room focused on Gage's table.

Grandpa Buck started to say something, but Gage cut him right off. "No, sir, just anxious for the auction to begin."

"Damn straight," Buck said.

The room erupted with laughter.

"Well, then, let's get on with it."

"This ought to be interesting," a man at the next table offered.

Grandma May seemed as if she was about to jump across the table and attack the man, but Cori held her down. "It's going to be fine."

"Let the games begin," an older man said. He sat at the table directly in front of them.

Gage looked to Cori for assurance, and instead she merely shrugged, giving him a queasy feeling in the pit of his stomach.

Oh, yeah, everything was right on track…for a complete disaster.

THE AUCTION WAS practically an all-day affair, with many of the first-edition books going for close to a thousand dollars each, depending on its condition and whether or not the dust jacket had some wear. So far, Gage had been able to outbid the entire room for most of the books he'd wanted, leaving everyone frustrated by his unabashed hoarding.

"There's only one thing I want," Cori's gram told her. "I want that Hardy-Zane reel, and his reed fishing pole. Zane liked to fish just like your grandpa did. Of course, Zane could afford a lot of poles and reels and he fished all over the world. Your gramps only fished in local streams and rivers. As long as he had his Zane Grey angler, he'd catch enough trout and bass to last us weeks at a time. Your gramps used to own one almost exactly like the one going up for auction."

"What happened to the one Gramps owned?"

"I had to sell it. Needed the money after your grandpa passed."

"Why didn't you tell me you were having financial problems? I would've been happy to help."

Gram gave her a hug. "I know, but your grandpa and me liked to do things for ourselves. I think you might know something about that kind of self-reliance. Never took a dime from your own parents after Hailey's dad passed. Always wanted to do it on your own. Still do. I've learned since then that sometimes it's good to ask for help, good to lean on somebody else for support. Makes us stronger."

Cori stopped herself from countering, thinking that her grandmother might be right. They'd both been so stubborn about standing on their own two feet that sometimes Cori had inadvertently alienated some of her friends and family members who had offered assistance. And Cori had gone even further and closed off her heart to the potential of loving another man. She'd taken on extra hours, so she didn't have to think about her loneliness, and substituted time with her daughter with time with her patients. And in the end, everyone suffered, especially her sweet daughter.

She glanced at Gage, wondering if she could ever lose her heart to a man like him, a man who struggled with alcohol and had a money addiction and an estranged family. Who could ride a horse as good as any cowboy, make her smile for almost no reason, took the time to escort his grandfather to the conference, and was winning her daughter's respect.

Could she fall for this man?

"Next up I have one of Zane Grey's anglers, complete with a Hardy-Zane reel. I'm starting the bid at one-thousand. Who will bid one thousand?"

Buck held up his numbered paddle, and a couple seconds later Cori's gram held up her paddle and said, "One thousand two hundred."

"I have one thousand two hundred for Zane's rod and reel," the president said in response.

"Two thousand," an older man with thick gray hair called out from a table in front of them.

"Two thousand one hundred," Buck yelled, holding up his paddle.

Instantly, Cori's gram called out another two hundred, then Buck countered with three hundred more and it went back and forth until the bid reached twenty-nine hundred dollars, with both Cori's gram and Buck standing and glaring at each other.

Cori knew how much her Gram wanted the angler,

but she also knew that twenty-nine hundred dollars was way too much money for her gram to dole out.

"Three thousand dollars," Cori yelled, thinking that would put an end to it, and for a while it did. The room fell silent but for the president. "I have three thousand dollars, going once, going..."

"Three thousand two hundred," Gage declared, holding up his paddle.

"Three thousand three hundred," Cori shouted.

"Four thousand dollars," Gage countered.

Cori was about to bid when her grandmother stopped her. "No, Corina-May. That's too much, and Buck's grandson won't stop. I don't want it if it's going to be like this. Let them have the dang thing."

"Four thousand going once," the president said.

"Gram, let me do this for you."

Gram placed her paddle down on the table. "I don't want it and if you keep this up, I won't forgive you for being so foolish with your hard-earned money." Then she folded her arms and sat back on the chair.

Cori knew her grandmother well enough that if she kept up the bidding war, she'd never hear the end of it. She had no choice but to relent to Gage.

"Going twice... Sold to number fifty-four."

"Yes!" Gage said, looking all proud of himself, patting the table, then making a fist and punching air. Cori could see him buying and selling millions of dollars' worth of commodities on the trading floor with nothing more than a hand gesture. The man was truly obsessed with the win, and nothing else seemed to matter, not even the effect he was having on Cori or her gram.

Cori overheard Buck say, "I hope you know that's yours, son. I told you not to get involved. This was something I wanted to do on my own. There's no limits on you, is there?" He stood. "Dang fool."

"We'll talk about it later, Gramps. Right now, we need to celebrate our win," Gage mumbled as the president went on to auctioning a large movie poster from the nineteen forty-one Zane Grey movie *Western Union*.

"Ain't gonna be no discussion," Buck said, then quickly left the table before Hailey brought over the rod and reel and handed it to Gage, who accepted the contested prize, thanking Hailey as she turned and skipped back to the stage. She was doing a great job handing out the auctioned merchandise, and Cori gave her a little smile and nod as she went by.

"You two ruined everything," Grandma May said as she followed right behind Buck. "I hope you're happy."

Her comments caught Cori by complete surprise. She knew her grandmother was upset with Gage, but she had no idea her dissatisfaction included Cori's behavior as well. Cori was merely doing what she thought would please her grandmother.

"But Gram, I…"

May strutted past Cori and never looked back.

"Going once. Going twice. Sold to number eighty-three for fifty dollars."

THE REMAINDER OF the auction went by in a blur as Gage reveled in every win. Cori acknowledged his victories, but never really gave him another glance, even though he'd tried on several occasions to get her attention. He'd allowed her to win a first edition of *Betty Zane*, and he'd stepped back when a small movie poster went up for auction of *The Last Trail*. And he hadn't bid at all when an autographed picture of a middle-aged Zane

Grey went up for auction and sold to a colorful woman with bright red hair at the next table.

When the auction ended and Gage walked up to the women who collected the money, he noticed that Cori hung back in line and didn't seem to want to talk to him, which was fine by him. The auction had showed her true colors. She'd known how much he wanted to impress his grandfather, yet she still bid on the one thing his grandfather really wanted and drove the price up to an absurd amount.

"It's all in good fun, right?" he said as she finally approached the front of the line. He'd waited for her after paying for the rod, reel, several first-edition books and a poster.

"If you say so," she said, without looking at him. As if she had something to be angry about. He was the one that should be carrying the grudge, yet there he was, being a gentleman.

He bent over to try to get her to look at him, which she would not. "Are you angry?"

"Hurt, more than anything else." Her expression reminded him of his wife when she had asked for a divorce, completely stoic. As if they had no history together. Granted, he and Cori shared only a two-day history, but still, did she have to be so cold?

"It's an auction. The guy with the most money wins."

"I know, but my gram really wanted that rod and reel."

"So did my gramps, and you know how I'm trying to get on his good side."

Cori handed the woman seated at the table a credit card. "That's not what I overheard. It sounded more like he was angry that you bought it for him."

She had a point. However, he was counting on a different outcome once his gramps held it in his hands, and the reality sunk in that he now owned one of Zane's original fishing anglers.

"That can't be true. You must not have heard him correctly. He's thrilled. I'm sure of it." The woman swiped Cori's card on a mobile credit card reader attached to a tablet, and seconds later Cori was signing her name on the small screen. Gage had done the same thing only a few minutes before. The line was moving quickly due to modern technology. Even though most everyone at the conference was in their golden years, none of them seemed to lack knowledge in the high-tech world. Even his gramps owned the latest smartphone.

"Maybe so, but I think we should keep our distance from now on. Nothing good can come from our attempt at being friends. It only leads to bad feelings."

Her words stung, especially after the previous night, when they'd had such a good time together. Still, if that was how she wanted to play it, then fine. He hadn't liked how selfish and uncaring she'd been about the auction, anyway.

"It's probably easier on both of us if we don't get involved."

She looked him in the eyes. "Who said anything about getting involved? I was referring to a possible friendship. Nothing more."

"Of course. That's exactly what I was referring to, our friendship," Gage said, wondering why she would go to such extremes over losing the bid. It smacked of being a sore loser, a vice she should have learned to overcome when she was Hailey's age.

"Perfect. Then we've agreed not to be friends."

"Yes. I mean no. I mean, we are not now and never will be friends. If that's how you want it." He knew she was angry over the loss of the fishing rod, but this new attempt at total isolation from one another during the remainder of the conference seemed ridiculous, especially since she knew as well as he did there was a chemistry between them that couldn't be denied.

"Me? I'm not the one who acted like a pompous ass. Just because you're part of the one percent, you don't have to flaunt it in everyone's face."

"Believe me, I'm a long way from being part of the one percent. And what if I was? Why is that a bad thing? Doesn't everyone want to be rich?"

She retrieved her credit card, shoved it into her purse, picked up the books and posters she'd purchased and headed for the door without saying another word. Gage followed right behind her, juggling his bounty in his arms.

"That's not the point. This is why we can't be friends. You can't even stay on topic." She picked up her pace still walking in front of him.

"Wait. What?"

Once they reached the exit, she stopped abruptly to face him. "What part of 'we should keep our distance' don't you understand? I've made myself perfectly clear."

One of the books slipped from his grasp and tumbled to the floor. He looked down to see a smiling cowboy looking back up at him, and in that instant he knew he'd slipped back into that Wall Street tiger who had to win, no matter what the cost. He'd awoken that morning thinking this kind of behavior was under control, just like his drinking, but apparently he still had a long way to go.

Cori was right. He had acted exactly like a pomp-ous ass.

An older gentleman bent over and retrieved the book and stacked it on top of the other books Gage held on to.

"Thanks," he told the man, then returned his atten-tion to Cori, who was now headed for the hotel lobby.

"Cori, wait," he called out, but she kept right on walking, her tight bottom swaying with each step, her long dark hair catching the light as she passed under the chandeliers. This feud had to end. One minute they were talking and having fun, and the next they were ar-guing. Granted, he'd gone about it all wrong, but she, of all people, should appreciate why he had to buy the rod and reel for his grandfather. It served as the ultimate peace offering. Why couldn't she get that?

Cori passed by his grandfather, but didn't stop as she rounded the corner, walking out of sight. He'd glanced over at his gramps and caught the look he'd directed to Cori as he stood chatting with another man just up the two steps that led into the lobby. Gramps actually made eye contact with Cori as she passed and had offered her what seemed like an apologetic smile.

Gage halted in his tracks as everything he carried began to slip from his grasp. Then in one split second the books, poster and contested rod and reel slipped from his arms and landed on the wooden floor with a clatter so loud everyone gazed his way.

"That's not how to impress a fine woman like that," his grandfather all but whispered to him as Gage stacked up his books.

"I wasn't trying to impress her. She's a frustrating, bullheaded, opinionated bully and I'm done with her."

"No, you're not. She's under your skin, and if you

want to keep her interested, you gotta find some common ground, something that will charm her every time you two are together, not pull you apart." When Gage finally looked up, his grandfather's expression seemed to soften. "Son, I'd help you with that stack, but my back ain't what it used to be. 'Sides, for all the money you spent today you should'a got a box."

He held out the perfect-sized box for the items.

"Thanks," Gage told him, accepting the welcomed container, then placing it on the floor and carefully stacking up as many of his books as he could fit.

When he finished and they were all tucked inside, he hoisted the box up onto his shoulder, still unable to handle the fishing pole.

"Let me give you a hand with that," his grandfather offered, plucking the expensive item off the floor. "Old Zane sure knew fishing. I heard a couple of fellas say during the auction that if they had the choice, they'd rather spend the day fishing than make love to a woman. I don't know if that's the mark of a true adventurer or not."

"A little over-the-top by my standards."

"Mine too," his grandfather said, giving Gage a little nudge with his elbow.

Gage gazed over at his grandfather as they walked toward the lobby.

"How'd you do it?" Gage asked him.

"Do what?"

"Stay married to the same woman for all that time and still be crazy about her?"

"Ain't nothing to it when you love somebody and they love you right back. It's a natural kind of thing."

Gage speculated on how his grandma, Rose, ever

put up with him when he turned ornery. But then he remembered her kindness and generosity. Gage couldn't think of one time when his gramps raised his voice to Rose or said a harsh word.

"I love you, Gramps, but we can't be in the same room for more than a few minutes before we're arguing. Why is that?"

"I admit I've been a little rough around the edges since your grandma passed. Plus, it don't help that I got this internal sugar problem that keeps naggin' at me. But those are my problems. You've got a boat load of your own brewin', one of 'em being you don't seem to know when to let somethin' be. It takes a lot of love and patience to know when to stop pushin' and open your heart."

"I was only married for four years when my wife called it quits."

They kept walking, the box of memorabilia getting heavy on his shoulder.

"And you let her go?"

"You can't hold on to a woman who doesn't love you anymore."

"Seems to me you're the one who left her. It takes a lot for a woman to fall out of love with her man. They're more loyal than we are, and smarter most of the time."

"She asked for the divorce, not me."

"Because she knew you didn't love her. That short amount of time being married, letting her go that easy, you probably never did."

"So, okay, let's say I truly never loved her. How would I know the difference?"

"You know when it's true love 'cause you can't breathe without her. But lovin' a woman ain't always enough to keep her. You gotta know *how* to keep her lovin' you."

"Sounds impossible. What's the secret? How'd you and Grandma Rose keep it together for all those years?"

"With humor, compassion, encouragement, and if you're lucky…good-tastin' pie."

Gage felt certain he hadn't heard him correctly. "What was that last thing?"

"Pie."

Gage chuckled at the absurdity of the statement. "Any particular kind?"

"That's just it. We liked to try all sorts of pies. Some people travel to see the sights or to shop or to immerse themselves in a different way of life. We went for the pie."

"And that kept your marriage alive for sixty-some years?"

"Yep. Who don't like pie? I defy you to stay mad when you're eatin' a slice of warm apple pie with ice cream, or passion fruit cream pie with whipped cream and jelly beans. Found that one in a cookbook written by a ten-year-old girl. One of the best pies I ever tasted."

"Pie. That's one of the secrets to a good marriage?"

"Sure worked for me and my gal."

As they approached the crowded lobby and the elevator, Gage couldn't let his gramps go without one more question.

"So, you're telling me all I have to do to win Doctor Cori Parker's heart—if I actually wanted to win her heart, which at the moment seems impossible, even though you seem to think I still have a chance—you're saying if we ate pie together, we would fall in love."

Gramps stopped walking, turned and stared Gage in the eye, a curious expression on his weathered face.

"I'm right about you, son. You listen with your head and not your heart. You can't think outside that big-city box you're looking out of. Shame, 'cause I know you got the chaps to make a fine cowboy, if you only tried a whole lot harder."

Then Gramps placed the rod and reel under Gage's arm, pressed the up arrow for the elevator and ambled toward the woman with the snow-white hair who'd provided Gramps with her pink sweater to use as a pillow when he collapsed. She was standing next to Steve Curtis, who took her hand and guided her and Gramps out the double doors and into the late afternoon sun, laughing as they made their way down the stairs.

The elevator doors opened and Gage stepped inside, going over what his grandfather had said, and decided that staying happily married to the same person for more than sixty years seemed like a heck of a lot of work, especially since he didn't even like pie, passion fruit or otherwise.

Chapter Six

There were events that Cori simply did not want to participate in. The barn dance happened to be one of them. Hailey had more or less forced her into attending, despite her insistence that she was tired and wanted to rest in their room. Her excuse didn't hold water with her daughter.

"Aren't you glad you came? Who could miss a real barn dance?"

Cori couldn't remember ever telling Hailey anything about it.

"And I suppose Grammy filled you in on what a barn dance is all about?"

Hailey grinned and nodded. "Oh, Momma, I'm having such a good time. Can we stay right here in Durango for a while? If we did, I could take horseback riding lessons and learn how to ride like Gage. Could we stay, Mom? Please?"

Hailey skipped along the sidewalk between her mom and Gram, a big smile on her face. She had accumulated several Zane Grey movie posters, books and even a teddy bear, all courtesy of thankful auction attendees. At first, Cori thought it might be too much, but everyone had insisted she keep them for having done such a great job. Hailey had already started reading one of the books and had plans to sleep with the cuddly teddy bear.

"We can consider it, but I don't know if I could get a practice going here. It's a really small town, sweetie. And besides, it's fun now because of the conference. I have no idea how it would be when we were here by ourselves."

"I'd be a lot closer," Gram offered. It was the first full sentence she'd uttered to Cori since the auction. "I thought you needed a change. Besides, I bet they could use a good doctor in this town. There can never be enough good doctors, especially doctors who care about their patients."

Cori wasn't quite ready to make a commitment to live anywhere but her grandmother's house for the near future, much less make a commitment to another practice. Sure, her gram's house was way too tiny, but in rethinking the situation, maybe she'd like to try something else entirely. Like maybe she'd write a book—a mystery or a steamy romance. If she couldn't have a sex life of her own, perhaps she could invent one in a novel. She needed to care about something again. Aside from Buck, she hadn't really cared about a patient in a very long time. He'd been the first patient in several years she'd allowed herself to feel something for. When you worked in an ER there was no time to get involved. You saw the patient once, handled the trauma and walked away. She'd practiced showing adequate compassion, but deep inside she'd kept her distance. It was merely part of the job. In some ways, that distance she continually practiced had somehow contributed to her chronic fatigue.

"I stopped really caring a long time ago, Gram."

"That's not true. I saw how you doted over that old fool, Buck Remington. You were kind and compassionate. No doubt more than he deserved, but it just goes to prove if you can feel sympathy for that old goat, your bedside manner hasn't changed since you took care of your grandfather."

"That was different."

Cori had flown in every weekend for eight months straight to take her grandfather to chemotherapy on Monday morning. He'd been so scared of the chemicals going into his body and what his reaction would be that she thought being there and explaining everything to him could ease his anxiety. She'd take him out to his favorite restaurant afterward, and the three of them would spend the night playing cards and watching old movies until he fell asleep in his recliner. Tuesday morning, bright and early, she'd be on a plane heading back to New York City and work the late shift. Hailey stayed at her best friend Susan's house for most of the weekends. She'd bring Hailey along sometimes, when her great-grandpa was feeling better, but for the most part Cori would go alone.

Cori didn't know what she would have done without Susan's parents, and even now the thought of moving away from such a strong support group seemed next to impossible.

"You just need a little time off to regroup. Everybody does at some point in their working career. It's normal. There's always a time when life starts to close in on us and we need to find our path all over again. You're in one of those times. Nothing to get overly concerned about. When you come out on the other end, you'll be stronger for it, and more confident in your life's work. I guarantee it."

They'd reached the Elks Lodge, a large two-story tan brick building where the barn dance would take place. One of the few places in town that had a wooden dance floor large enough to hold everyone.

"You should listen to Grammy, Mom. She's smart," Hailey chimed in as she swung open the heavy door, grunting and trying with all her might to keep it open.

"Here, let me get that for you," Gage said from behind Cori, then he reached over her head and grabbed the awkward door. He stood only a heartbeat away from her, causing her to want to move out of the way, but she couldn't. She was trapped between her daughter and the door.

The sound of his voice had startled her as she'd pulled in a breath. How long had he been following them? Had he heard their conversation? Cori wanted to die right there in front of the Elks Lodge, but there was nowhere to land when life slipped from her body other than his waiting arms.

"Thanks," Hailey said, obviously tickled to see him. "I was hoping you'd be here. I want to be the first person to ask you to dance. I bet you know all about the two-step and line dancing."

"It's been awhile," Gage answered, as everyone made their way through the door. "But, just like riding a horse, I'm sure it will come back to me." He chuckled as Hailey took his hand and hurried him into the next room where the band had already started the hootenanny.

"She likes him," Gram said, without a trace of malice. "And, despite his being an ornery Remington, I think you do too."

"I have absolutely no interest in Gage Remington. He's exactly everything I dislike in a man. He's arrogant, obtrusive and a total pain with an addictive personality. Once this conference is over, I never have to see him again as long as I live, because he certainly won't be escorting his grandfather to one of these events in the future. Not after his shenanigans at the auction today. The man has no sense of decorum. He's an absolute boor."

Gram gazed at Cori as she hurried to get into the other room. Real cowboy music was her favorite, and from what Cori could make out, it was happening in the next room. "If all that's true, sweetheart, how do you explain the flush on your pretty face?"

Cori's hands instantly covered her cheeks, mortified that she'd had such a visceral reaction to being close to him when logic dictated the opposite. Could she be that powerless in her resolve?

She stopped in the doorway that led into the dance hall knowing full well that reason told her she should turn right around and return to the hotel, but when she saw big, hunky Gage Remington teaching petite Hailey Parker the two-step, all her apprehensions completely melted away.

Oh, yeah, she had it bad.

Gage hadn't been to a real barn dance since he was ten and even then, he'd never appreciated the music as much as he did now. It was lively and upbeat, earthy and downright American. Nothing pretentious. It was all about having fun and it didn't matter what your clothes looked like, where you were from or the color of your skin. Everyone was there to have a good time. Check your ego at the door and allow yourself at least one good "yee-haw" during the night, and everything would be all right.

Exactly what he needed.

The room vibrated with stomping boots, hoots and whistles as the band belted out one classic country song after another, by artists Gage had all but forgotten. One of the more amazing components of the band happened to be that not one of them was over twenty-five. Six people comprised the band—four young men and two young women. Of the two women, wearing black fringed skirts, red Western shirts and black boots, one played a guitar and the other the banjo. The four cowboys, wearing Western hats, shirts with embroidered detail, jeans and boots, played an accordion, a bass fiddle and two red-hot violins.

The music was lively and plentiful, which kept the crowd of Zane Grey fans on the dance floor.

As the night wore on and Hailey took what Gage had taught her and danced with just about everyone, he realized the one person he wanted to hold in his arms had purposely ignored him, which he had expected and was fine with. Still, he couldn't help wondering what holding Cori close would feel like. He knew she didn't want anything to do with him, yet he'd catch her looking over at him as if she had second thoughts about the whole friend routine.

The woman drove him to distraction.

He wanted the night to be over, and if he hadn't promised Hailey the last dance, he would be back in his room reading one of the books he'd purchased that afternoon. Instead, here he was torturing himself over whether or not he should ask Cori to dance.

Not that he would, knowing how she felt about their

situation, but he liked to contemplate the idea. It gave him something to focus on while he indulged at the dessert table and enjoyed several glasses of sparkling apple cider.

On the other hand, his grandfather's silence during the entire evening was something else entirely.

He'd made countless attempts to chat with Gramps, but the man would have none of it. He thought they had come to some sort of terms that afternoon, but apparently those terms still needed negotiating. Gage even brought him an assortment of tasty treats from the dessert table, only to be reprimanded for his efforts.

"You know I can't eat those in my condition. Are you trying to kill me?" Gramps protested over the music.

"No. I... Of course not. I just thought, well, I don't know what I thought...a peace offering?"

"It ain't me you need to be making peace with. At least, not now. You gotta work on your timin', son. I'm gonna get in that there line and do a little dancin'. I suggest you get rid of them cookies and do the same. Go get that girl you been soft on and ask her for a dance like I taught you. Or did you forget all your cowboy ways, livin' in that big city?"

"No. I remember everything you taught me."

Gramps gave him the once over. "Then start actin' like it."

Gage watched as Gramps slid onto the dance floor and merged into one of the lines like a pro. He and his grandmother had loved to dance, and Gage had countless memories of spirited barn dances with not only his grandparents but also his parents. Those summers on the ranch were the only times he'd ever seen his parents dance.

Gage had done his share of clubbing in New York City, but those nights usually ended in a drunken blur. "Brownies? Cookies? Seriously?" Cori said as she approached. He welcomed her sudden appearance, albeit to critique his ridiculous gesture. He loved that she'd worn that same purple skirt and the Western boots she'd worn on their dinner date. This time she swapped out the red blouse with a formfitting Western-type one that showed just the right amount of cleavage.

Did she know the affect she was having on him, or was she completely oblivious to his attraction?

Hoots and laughter echoed throughout the room, along with syncopated pounding from a lot of boots hitting the wooden dance floor. Everyone seemed to be having a good time—everyone except Gage. He couldn't catch a break…at least not until Cori stopped by.

"I needed to do something to break the ice with him. I guess sugary desserts weren't exactly the icebreaker I had hoped for."

He plunked the plate down on one of the many tables that surrounded the dance floor, each one covered by a red checkered table cloth. Two large dessert stations had been set up at the back of the room, along with a drink station that served only non-alcoholic beverages. Gage had already downed his share of sparkling cider and soda water and wished like hell he could have a couple shots of bourbon to help him get through the remainder of the evening.

"You should dance with Gage, Mom," Hailey insisted as she rushed up to them. "He taught me everything I know, and I've been dancing all night."

"Oh, I don't…" Cori said.

"Don't you want to dance, Mom? It's so much fun."

"Well, sweet pea, Gage hasn't asked me."

"I didn't think you would want to," Gage said.

"I don't," Cori snapped, then started to walk away, until her grandmother stopped her.

"Corina-May, you haven't been on that dance floor all night. It's not healthy for you not to whoop it up at least once in a while."

Gage caught up to Cori, and with all the graciousness his grandparents had taught him he said, "Doctor Cori Parker, nothing would give me more pleasure than to have you dance with me."

A slow warm smile slipped across her full lips as Gage patiently waited for what he hoped would be a positive reply.

"I'd love to, but I don't know how to line dance."

"It's easy, Mom," Hailey said as she slipped in front of Cori.

"I can teach you. We'll take it nice and slow," Gage assured her.

Gage wanted to keep his distance, so he figured line dancing would be a safe choice.

"I have two left feet."

He gazed down at her boots. "They look normal enough to me."

"I...I..."

The song ended with a cheer, and one of the women onstage made an announcement, "We had a request to slow it down a bit, so we thought we'd do one of our favorite Patsy Cline tunes. Hope you like it."

"Now you can't say no, Momma. I know you know how to slow dance. You used to dance with Daddy in our kitchen all the time."

"You remember that?"

Hailey's dad had loved to dance, especially a waltz. Whenever a slow song came on the radio, wherever they were, he'd take her in his arms and they'd dance. It didn't matter if they were in a store, out on the sidewalk, in a restaurant or in the car, he'd have to dance with her. It was one of his most endearing qualities, and Cori was so happy that Hailey had kept that memory.

"Uh-huh," Hailey said, nodding. "I used to dance on Daddy's feet. He taught me all about slow dancing."

Cori squatted in order to be level with Hailey, then she hugged her. "Don't you ever forget that, okay?"

When they parted, Hailey said, "How could I forget? It's locked up in my brain with all the rest of the junk I remember."

Gage's eyes watered imagining a much younger Hailey and her daddy dancing together while Cori stood back and absorbed the moment. He was beginning to understand how that kind of loss could devastate a family. Being sober put him in touch with his emotions and even though it was sometimes painful, he felt more alive than he had in a very long time.

"But that's a special memory. One that you'll want to retrieve when you're my age and you're reminiscing about your daddy."

"Do you have those kinds of memories about Daddy?"

"Yes, and I put them in a very special place in my heart."

"Don't be silly, Momma. Our hearts can't remember things."

"Sure they can. It's where we store all our love moments."

"Okay." She closed her eyes tight for a few seconds and when she opened them again, she said, "I just locked it away in my heart forever, but it's going to get really crowded in there with all my love moments. I already have so many I can't keep track of them, and I'm just a kid. What'll happen by the time I get as old as you?"

"You'll be able to buy more space on the internet," May said, breaking in on the moment. "Now let's you and me dance and leave your Momma and Gage to their own devices."

May pulled Hailey out on the floor just as the lead singer crooned the first line of "I Fall to Pieces."

Gage held out his hand for Cori. "This one's ours," he said.

Her smile deepened and her eyes sparkled as she reached out for his hand. "You know I'm still angry about the auction."

"I'm not asking you to forgive me. I'm asking you to dance with me."

He gestured toward the dance floor.

"Just this once," she told him, but he could tell she wasn't being truthful.

"That'll do for now."

Within a few breathless seconds, they stepped on the wooden floor and he held her wrapped in his arms. The smell of her perfume clouded his thinking, and when she leaned in against him, he knew this was one of those special moments he would tuck away in his heart forever.

CORI NEVER ANTICIPATED what a roller coaster of emotions she would feel while dancing with Gage, especially since she now knew about his addiction to alcohol. Dancing with him, being so close to him that she rested her head on his shoulder tore at her emotions. Part of her knew better than to play with fire, and Gage was most certainly fire. How could he be anything else? The man was a recovering alcoholic, and he hadn't been recovering for very long. The odds were not in his favor. She knew the statistics and had done extensive research when her husband had been killed by a drunk driver. The accident had spared the driver's girlfriend, who'd been a passenger in the car, but that wasn't the case for the guy behind the wheel. He had died at the scene, along with Cori's husband.

Statistics showed that an educated man like Gage was more prone to drink alcohol again in a social environment, thinking he could handle it and the majority of alcoholics could not.

Five years seemed to be the magic amount of time for someone in recovery. If the person made it to the five-year mark, the chances of him or her returning to alcohol were almost nonexistent. The driver who had killed her husband had been sober for more than four years. He and his girlfriend had been out celebrating the grand opening of his new restaurant in SoHo with a bottle of wine that she claimed he hardly drank. The autopsy showed his BAC was two times the legal limit.

That woman nearly lost her life that night because she believed her boyfriend "hardly drank," when in fact he had consumed enough wine to allow him to drive on the wrong side of the road.

Cori wondered if she would be that naive. Could she believe in Gage's sobriety long enough to wait and see if he stayed sober, or would she be checking up on him every time alcohol was anywhere near him?

Or was this simply a vacation romance and nothing

more? She could handle a fling, a tryst, a no-strings-attached kind of romance. Maybe she'd been looking at the situation all wrong. Just because she was attracted to Gage didn't mean she had to be thinking about their long-term future together.

She wasn't falling in love with the man. She was merely tempted by him…and heaven help her, the temptation was all-consuming. Especially now, while they were dancing so close she could feel his hard body under the thin fabric of his shirt.

Still, she had to tell him all that she was thinking, all her concerns and fears. He was a smart man. He had to understand that whatever they were feeling for each other could only be played out while they were in Durango, and even then, it had to be done discreetly. Neither of their grandparents could know, nor could Hailey—especially Hailey, who seemed to be attaching herself to Gage. She couldn't allow that to happen.

They had to keep their tryst secret and only while they were in Durango. If he agreed, they wouldn't have to discuss any of her concerns over his future drinking, because they wouldn't have a future. They would only have now.

This moment.

In this town.

"Can we go somewhere quiet?" she asked as she gazed into his smoky eyes.

He pulled back to look at her. "Now?"

But she couldn't quite answer. Instead she fell deeper into those eyes of his, wondering what it would be like to make love to him, to have his strong arms wrapped around her while they were naked, lying in bed.

She pushed the vision away. "Um, yes, I think it's important. I have something I need to say."

He was staring at her, his gaze sliding down to her lips and lingering there until she could barely breathe. The song wasn't helping her to concentrate on what she wanted to say.

"What is it?" he said it in a deep whisper, and that vision of them naked in bed came rushing back.

"I want to tell you…"

His fingers wrapped tighter around her hand as he pulled her in closer and rested her hand on his upper chest. Her thoughts seemed muddled and confused.

"You can tell me anything."

"I can?"

"Yes, anything."

They spun around a couple times causing her world to spin as she sunk in closer to him.

His warm breath felt like silk brushing her skin. "You were saying?"

"Was I speaking?"

He smiled, and his thumb ran across the inside of her palm, right when the singer let loose with the song's refrain.

Oh, yeah, she was falling, all right—into a million tiny pieces.

"I believe you were. Yes."

The heat between them slid through her body and surrounded them with an intensity that could explode into flames if she wasn't careful. As long as she was in his arms, there was little hope she could act or speak with any sense of reason. The only thing she could think to say was *let's go back to your room and make love*.

Fortunately, the song ended, he took a step back, dropping his embrace and she came to her senses.

"I'm thinking we should have a hookup."

"A what?"

"A hookup. Isn't that what sex between friends is called these days?"

"Let's get out of here," he murmured and grasped her hand.

A chill rushed up her spine and she was just about to agree when the music started up again and a Texas Star Square Dance began, complete with calls. Hailey and Gram hurried to join them, along with Steve Court and his wife, Betsy, who Gage seemed to already know. Then a third couple joined the group just as the dance began. The two new couples knew all the calls and led everyone with the correct formations. The band played the music while one of the cowboys crooned out the instructions.

"Join hands and circle to the left."

"Gents go in with a right hand star."

"Now left hand back."

"All four ladies...."

The caller went on for at least ten minutes. Keeping up with the right steps and moves turned out to be a challenge for Cori, but to her amazement Gage had no problems at all. He seemed to know exactly what to do.

"You know how to square dance, too?" Cori asked as they did a short promenade to the left, then to the right.

"My grandma Rose taught me," he said with a grin.

"This is crazy. You really are a cowboy."

"Only on occasion."

"All four ladies go into the middle, then back to the barn."

"I'm glad I'm part of the occasion."

"And gents go in with a right-hand star."

Gage danced to the middle but fastened his gaze on Cori.

When the caller sang, *"Couple number two go right on through the door,"* everyone grasped hands and danced through the circle.

"Was that a compliment?"

"Couple three go right on through."

When they passed each other, Cori said, "Yes. I believe it was."

"Well, I'll be danged," Gage said, hesitating for a moment only to get pulled back into his spot by Hailey.

The dance continued, with Cori getting all tangled up every now and then, feeling like she truly did have two left feet. Fortunately, Gage seemed to be there each time to untangle her and keep her moving. She actually loved the dance and wished she knew the steps better. Between the music, the caller, learning a new dance and her latest decision, happiness simmered inside her, escaping through a chronic smile that was beginning to hurt her cheeks.

Then, just as she thought she would pass out from trying to keep up with the caller, he sang those blessed words.

"That's all there is, there ain't no more."

The room exploded with cheers and whistles. Even Cori let go of a loud *woo-hoo!*

Gram had been right.

She needed to whoop it up, and what better way than to whoop with Gage Remington?

Chapter Seven

"I've given this some thought, and if you agree, I think it might be beneficial to us both," Cori explained as she and Gage slowly made their way over to the hotel. It was going on ten thirty and everyone had hustled back to their rooms as soon as the dance was over, including Cori's gram and Hailey. Gage was still trying to come to terms with Cori's hookup announcement as they left the dance. Not that he was in the least bit opposed to the idea. He simply never saw her as the casual-sex type. Why the sudden change of heart?

He knew they had shared some major heat during that slow song, but the square dance had interrupted what would have certainly ended in an unforgettable night.

"We're an us?"

"Yes."

"But just this afternoon you told me, and I quote, 'we should keep our distance.'"

One thing about Doctor Cori Parker, she knew how to dangle him on the line. Not that he minded it, exactly, but he sure wished she'd stick with a decision.

"I was wrong and you were right. We should be

friends. We're both in flux right now with our lives, so friends seems like the logical way to go."

He didn't know if he could trust her. She changed her course more than a New Yorker driving through midtown during rush hour. He wanted detailed facts.

"What kind of friends?"

They had stopped walking and stood standing in front of one of the Western apparel shops in the town. "Close…friends."

"How…close?"

"I don't know. Close, you know, close friends."

She began walking again.

"The benefits type of close friends or the friends-friends type?"

She took in a deep breath and let it out, gazed down at the sidewalk and then turned to him. "The hookup, benefits kind."

He moved in closer, and couldn't help but smile. "All benefits?"

"Yes, but I have my terms."

"Terms?"

"This benefits thing is only for while we're here in Durango. It can't go on afterward."

Those terms he could abide by. Once he was back in New York his focus would be on his family and saving his job. It sounded harsh, but he was glad she'd understand.

"That's fair. Anything else?"

"Our families can't know. I don't want Hailey or my gram to know we're…you know."

"Enjoying our benefits?"

Never had any woman intrigued him as much as Doctor Cori Parker. Not only was he fascinated by her easy relationship with her daughter, but the fact that she had worked in an emergency room and saved lives blew his world apart. His life had consisted of making money and getting drunk. Everything else was merely icing. Cori's life meant something significant to a lot of people. His life had been, well, less than what he had imagined it would be when he had gazed up at all those stars from his grandparents' ranch. He truly wanted to change all that, and spending time with Cori, either in the bedroom or on a dance floor, would certainly be the best first step he could ever take.

Nothing came easy in this relationship. They couldn't just fall into bed together—there had to be rules. Because he'd won that darn fishing rod when her grandmother had wanted it, they couldn't be friends, but now they were going to be friends with benefits, a hookup. The woman never ceased to surprise him. Each day brought a new adventure. From the moment he'd met her, something told him he should walk away, but he couldn't then, and he certainly couldn't now. "Yes."

"Not a problem. I'd rather they didn't know, especially with all the animosity going on between our grandparents."

They passed a few of the conference attendees. Everyone exchanged greetings and went on their way. A few other people—mostly younger men and women—were out and about, but for the most part the town seemed fairly deserted.

"I especially don't want Hailey to think this is an ongoing relationship or that her mother sleeps around."

"I understand."

He did understand that a person's private life deserved to be kept private, but he had to admit his pride was a bit wounded. He liked Hailey, and he didn't like the idea of not being totally upfront with her, even if it was at her mother's request.

"Okay, then we have an agreement? Can we shake on it?" She stopped walking and held out her hand.

"I'd rather kiss on it, if you don't mind."

"Someone might see us."

"We're still blocks from the hotel, the streets are dark and I'm sure all the older folks are heading for their beds. I refuse to agree to anything of this nature without a kiss."

He moved in closer to her, their lips only a whisper away from each other. "What kind of kiss? Short or long?" she asked.

"Does it matter?"

"Yes, I…"

But before he allowed her to say another word his lips had claimed hers.

CORI COULDN'T HELP HERSELF. She'd forgotten what it was like to be kissed like that. His mouth on hers was like heaven. His kiss awakened desires she had purposely stopped fantasizing about. She'd learned to accept there might not ever be another man in her life, until she met Gage. There had been something about him from their first hello that had drawn her in, and now that she was in his arms, it seemed right. As if this had been planned from the start.

They kissed under the streetlight, then while leaning against a storefront, then on a bench, a step, and inside a darkened doorway of a closed dress shop. His hands slipped over her breasts several times, making her want him more than she'd ever thought possible.

"You know, I have a private room at the hotel," he told her, only steps from the entrance. "We could explore those benefits right now."

"Sounds delightful," she told him without hesitation.

They just about ran the rest of the way to the hotel. When they arrived breathless in the lobby, Cori didn't want to take any chances that there might be someone hanging around who would report back to their grandparents, so they strolled in side by side, casually chatting about the barn dance. A conference of this size with only about seventy-five attendees where almost everyone knew each other was like living in a close-knit neighborhood for a few days. Cori usually liked that kind of camaraderie, but because of the nature of her new relationship with Gage, and with their grandparents discouraging any kind of real contact between them, knowing they'd decided to enjoy a benefits-type of connection might be what tipped Gage's grandfather away from him for good. And Cori's grandmother might never forgive her.

The old-fashioned lobby, with its paisley carpet and early American sofas, was empty except for two young men handling the front desk.

Everyone exchanged a friendly "good night" as Cori and Gage passed by the desk and headed for the elevator. As soon as they stepped into the elevator and the doors closed, Gage reached over and pulled Cori to him, one hand tangled in her hair while Cori wrapped a leg around his leg. He moved her thigh and pulled her in tighter until she pressed her body against his. Heat and desire took over and she could barely stand.

Just before the doors opened they managed to stop kissing. She ran a hand through her tousled hair and shifted away from him. When the doors parted, Gage gestured for her to step out first, with him following right behind.

As soon as they turned the corner for his room, Grandpa Buck nearly bumped right into her coming up the hallway. She froze for a moment, not knowing which way to go.

"You two just gettin' in?" he asked with a grin.

"Yep. Cori wanted to stop for ice cream," Gage said, trying to sound convincing.

"Huh. I didn't know the ice-cream shop was open this late."

"It isn't. We went for a wagon ride afterward," Cori added, hoping he'd buy it and stop asking questions.

"Can't get enough, huh? Didn't you two take a ride last night?" Cori started to question how he knew, but then remembered that almost nothing got past this group. She only hoped she and Gage could manage to keep their hookup secret, at least until it was time to leave.

"We did, and had so much fun we thought we'd do it again," Gage explained, but Cori could tell he was getting impatient.

"So what did you two think about the barn dance tonight? Fun?"

Cori couldn't believe Buck wanted to have a conversation this late. Weren't most people his age fast asleep by now? She knew her gram was.

"A hoot!" Gage said a little too quickly.

Buck turned to Cori. "Isn't your room on the second floor?"

She had to think fast. Buck was simply much too observant. She spotted the coffee and hot water station perched on top of an antique dresser. "Yes, it sure is, but there's no hot water in the thermos on my floor so I came up here to see if there was still some left. I like a hot cup of herbal tea before bed."

Not entirely a lie. There were times when she enjoyed herbal tea before bedtime. She couldn't think of when those times might be at the moment, but she was sure she had imbibed at some point in her life. To make her story seem more believable, she went over to the beverage station and started preparing the tea.

A room door opened and an older woman, wearing a pink fuzzy robe and slippers walked out. "I heard voices out here. Oh, hi, Buck. That was some barn dance tonight, wasn't it? My name's Ruth, I don't think we've been officially introduced, yet."

The woman stepped forward and offered her hand to Cori.

"Hi, I'm Doctor Cori Parker," she said, shaking Ruth's hand.

"You're the doctor Buck's been talking about. Heard a lot about you. Saw you dancing tonight with this young fella." She nodded toward Gage.

He shook the woman's hand. "Gage Remington, Buck's grandson."

"Nice to meet you," Ruth said, then she leaned in and whispered, "Buck's quite a character."

Gage agreed as another door opened and a man with graying hair walked out, wrapped in a flannel robe with a woman still in her street clothes by his side.

Soon everyone with a room on the third floor was out in the hallway talking about the dance, the conference and Zane Grey's books. Cori and Gage had no choice but to join in on the conversations, which lasted for at least another forty-five minutes.

"Well," Cori finally said with a little yawn as Buck and Gage were just getting into an intense discussion on Zane Grey's *Heritage of the Desert*. They sat on the sofa near the elevator sipping hot herbal tea, Gage apparently enjoying the discussion of one of his favorite books. Cori couldn't help but smile at the two of them actually having a civil conversation. She knew how much Gage had longed for a moment like this.

"I think I'll be heading back to my room," she said. "We have an early day tomorrow."

Gage gave her a sorry look. "What time do we need to be at the station?"

"Seven," Buck told him, then he said goodnight to Cori and picked up where he'd left off in his debate with Gage.

Gage stood, ignoring his grandfather. "Can I walk you back to your room?"

"No, I'm good. It's only one floor down. Catch you in the morning," she told him, utterly disappointed their tryst had been interrupted.

"In the morning," he repeated, and as she made her way down the stairs she could hear Gage and Buck yammering on about a passage in the book. Buck tried to convince Gage that Zane Grey was also a romance writer, and the ending proved it.

Cori didn't know how the book ended, but she knew how her night had ended.

Alone, without any romance of any kind.

THE SUNLIGHT SEEMED extra harsh as Gage jogged the three or so blocks to the train station. He had to hustle due to the fact that he'd overslept. His grandfather had woken him in plenty of time, but Gage had said to go on without him and that he'd catch up.

Instead of waking up next to Cori, or at least waking up with memories of making love to Cori, he'd awoken with a dry throat from spending most of the night arguing with Buck over whether or not Zane Grey was actually a Western romance writer.

In the end they had agreed that Zane wrote romantic Westerns, a compromise he now wished they had found at midnight instead of two in the morning. If he didn't know for sure he hadn't drunk any liquor last night, he would swear the headache that pounded in the back of his skull was from booze. From now on, he assured himself, he was off sparkling apple juice as well as herbal tea.

When he rounded the corner for the train, the familiar whistle nearly blew his ears off. How he was going to deal with the combination of that piercing sound and the seven-thousand foot climb up the side of the mountain was a mystery, but he refused to miss one of his last two days with Cori.

He'd already decided that not even his grandfather, Cori's grandmother, their friends or even Hailey would stop them. Short of some earth-shattering catastrophe, he intended to make love with Cori that evening and nothing was going to get in their way.

He just needed a plan.

"Run!" Hailey yelled from inside one of the cars. "The train is leaving!"

She sat next to Cori in a covered train car. Gage hoped one of them had saved him a seat as he dashed across the lawn, up the brick walkway and climbed on-board their car just as the train started moving, steam and black smoke pouring from the engine up ahead.

Everyone in the car cheered and clapped.

"That was close," he said, chuckling. Even if he had missed the train, Gage would have found a way to get to Silverton if he had to rent a car or pay someone to take him.

"Saved you a seat," Gramps said as Gage gazed ahead at the empty seat next to Cori. Everything in him wanted to sit with Cori, but he knew he couldn't ignore his gramps.

"Thanks," he said and swung in next to his grandfather on the deep green leather seat. The Prospector Car had a mostly wooden interior with leather and steel. The car was a combination of new and refurbished parts. They sat around a low cocktail table across Ruth—the woman he'd met the previous night in the hallway—and her husband Fred, who were busy with their own private discussion.

Gage really did love old trains, and this one had to rank right up there with the best of them.

"I've been wanting to do this for a lot of years," Gramps said. "I'm glad I'm finally gettin' to do it with you, son."

Gage stared at him, thinking *who are you and what did you do with my grandfather?*

"Me too, Gramps." Gramps patted Gage on the thigh, just like he had whenever they drove somewhere together in the old ranch truck. That single gesture, a pat on the thigh, always told Gage that no matter what, his grandpa loved him. His grandma had told him that Buck wasn't much on saying what he felt. He was more about showing you. A pat on the back or the shoulder or the thigh was his way of showing his love and Gage never appreciated it more than that very moment.

Gage did the same gesture back on his grandfather's thigh, both men smiled at each other and then they turned to watch the scenery. It was another of those moments Gage would stow away in his heart.

Within ten minutes the train began its climb to Silverton, the old gold mining town nestled up in the mountains, and Gage decided to sit back, allow the aspirin he'd taken right before he left the hotel to take effect and enjoy the view of the San Juan Mountains and Forest along the way. The views were of spectacular canyons, streams and thick green forests, with high mountain peaks in the distance that were still covered with snow. At one point a guy on a zip line raced by in the distance, giving everyone a thrill.

The terrain changed to gray rocky hillsides as the train squeaked and swayed over a long bridge with a deep gorge on both sides. Then they slowly made their way around the side of a mountain, where Gage marveled at the technology that was used to carve out tracks through the rock.

What Gage loved most about being on the train was the constant rumble and churning of the wheels—that continual rocking, to and fro, that lulled all his tension and stress away. For what seemed like a long time, they ran right next to the rushing Animas River, its waters high and green as it tumbled on its way to the ocean. Gage could hear the water over the sound of the rumbling train, and the combination of the two only added to his love of the entire experience. He'd been looking forward to this ride, and so far it surpassed his imagination.

Whenever he gazed up ahead at Cori, who happened to be facing him, she would either be smiling in his direction or smiling at her grandmother or Hailey. His gaze kept drifting to those full ruby lips of hers and he couldn't help but think about last night. Those soft lips and her round breasts had ignited a flame deep within him that he'd thought had all but burned out.

He and Cori had only kissed, and he was already caught up in her charms. What the heck would it be like when they finally spent some real time getting to know each other?

She smiled over at him and he knew if he kept ruminating on his feelings for her, his comfort level on this train would be sorely compromised.

Still, he couldn't seem to let it go, so he asked his grandfather a simple question.

"Gramps, what are your thoughts on pie?"

AFTER THREE AND A HALF HOURS of swaying scenic beauty, the train made its final stop at the Silverton station. Everyone seemed anxious to exit and get to the town or a nearby restaurant for lunch. Cori was anxious to meet up with Gage. She'd spent the majority of her time trying not to stare over at him, but that sexy, teasing gleam in his eyes kept drawing her back for more.

The rest of her time was spent keeping up with the conversations between Hailey and Gram. At one point Gage had walked over to them for a short chat. Ironically, neither grandparent balked at the casual meeting. Gram all but ignored him, and Buck busied himself with a conversation between friends. No one stomped their feet or made a scene, which seemed a bit odd to Cori, but she let it pass.

Ironically, although this was early June, the altitude brought a chill to the air. Fortunately, Gram had packed sweaters and handed them out before they exited the train.

"I want to check out the shops," Gram said. "I didn't come all the way up here to sit in a restaurant. Besides, I ate enough protein bars on the train to last me for hours, so I'm good."

"Me, too," Hailey announced. "I want to buy Susan a souvenir. When I told her we were taking a train up a mountainside to a Silverton, she said she'd like something from the highest earthy place I've ever seen, just in case it looked different from normal places. But this town looks normal to me, except for the buildings. They look really old."

"Most of them are old, from the late eighteen hundreds." Cori tried to remember what she'd read about Silverton, but aside from the old bordellos that used to be on Blair Street and the jail and courthouse museums, there wasn't much to the tiny town.

"Still, I need to buy her something. I got twenty-five dollars for helping Gram in her garden in the backyard. I want to use some of it for Susan."

"Sounds like a plan. Let's go shopping," Cori agreed, while watching Gage and Buck exit the train and thinking how she wished she could text Gage and set up a meeting. Unfortunately, they hadn't exchanged phone numbers, and because of that oversight she had no way to contact him. Of course, neither one of them had had any idea the previous night would turn out the way it had.

"We're taking a group picture, so if everyone would please gather in front of the engine we can get it done quickly." The president, along with his wife, herded everyone forward. Cori felt this might be a prime opportunity to slip her phone number to Gage. She tore off a slip of paper from the small note pad she kept in her purse and found her pen.

As the group gathered in front of the impressive, hissing locomotive, Cori made her way over to Gage, who seemed to be heading her way as well. When they passed each other she slipped him the note.

"My number," she discreetly told him as he grabbed the paper.

"Mine, too," he said, and handed her a matchbook.

"This is ridiculous," Cori said.

"You don't have to be in the picture if you don't want to be," the president grumbled, as he passed by.

"I wasn't meaning..." But he kept right on walking and directing people to the front of their engine, number 480. It still spewed out white steam and black smoke.

Cori turned to Gage. "Now everyone will think I don't want to be in the picture. I'll never hear the end of it from my grandmother."

"I could kiss you right now and we'd really give them something to talk about," Gage offered, stepping in closer.

She pushed on his chest to hold him back. "You agreed not to tell anyone."

"I'm not telling, I'm showing. Big difference."

He pressed in harder on her hand, and she took a couple steps back, tripping over a railroad track. He quickly grabbed her so she wouldn't fall.

"Whoa," Gage said. "Watch your step."

"Careful there, Doc. You could hurt yourself," Buck warned. "Good thing Gage was here to catch you."

Buck had come up to stand next to Gage for the picture.

"Yes, a good thing," Cori repeated, hoping like heck Gage would back off.

"Timing's everything in this life," Gage said and let go of her. "Are you all right?"

"Fine," she told him, relieved that he'd decided to honor their agreement. He grinned and walked around to the other side of his grandfather, while Hailey and Gram walked over to Cori.

"Are you okay, Corina-May? What happened?" Gram asked.

"I'm fine. I tripped on the track."

"And Gage caught you. So far he's saved both of us, Momma. He's a real hero," Hailey said over the din of chatter as everyone tried to get into position for the group photo. "We should give him a medal or something."

"Or something," Cori said, not thinking anything of it until Gage smirked over at her.

Every time she was around him she could barely think, let alone do or say anything rational. She knew deep in her heart that she was falling for him, and if they went through with making love, she couldn't be sure her heart wouldn't break into a million pieces when she had to walk away from him.

But at this point, and after what she'd felt the previous night each time he kissed her, there was little hope she wouldn't go through with their agreement. She craved him more than she'd like to admit. Now all she had to do was figure out how that moment would come about.

As the group moved in tighter for the photo, Cori felt

a flush wash over her face. She wanted to get away from everyone. Instead, they kept encroaching on her space, making it difficult for her to keep her distance from Gage. She told herself to calm down, to take deep slow breaths, but for some reason being that close to him with everyone around was more than she could deal with.

"Hold on," Gage told her, as his hand slipped around her waist. "You're getting a bit wobbly."

"I need to sit down," she whispered, feeling a bit light-headed.

She knew she was experiencing a touch of altitude sickness. She needed to relax, to allow her body to get used to the height, and Gage standing next to her with his broad shoulders and chiseled face wasn't helping.

The picture-taking stopped and everyone began to disperse.

"Are you okay, Mom?" Hailey asked, looking scared, her thick caramel-colored hair falling around her face in loose curls and ringlets. "Is being so high up making you sick, Mom?" Cori felt certain her daughter was an old soul wrapped in a young girls' body. Cori had warned her about altitude sickness weeks ago when they were planning their trip.

"I'm fine, honey, I just need to sit down."

"Maybe you've got low blood sugar, like me. Get her some juice, son," Buck said to Gage.

"My granddaughter does not have low blood sugar, and if she did, she certainly doesn't need your advice," May snapped.

"He was just being helpful, Grammy," Hailey countered.

"Nobody needs you to stick your nose in where it ain't needed," Buck told May.

"She's my granddaughter, and I have a perfect right to stick my nose in wherever I want to," May announced, her face slightly red.

"Can everyone please calm down?" Gage interrupted, holding up his hands.

"I don't need to calm down. What I need is to get away from this here woman who makes my blood boil," Buck argued. "Are you coming, son?"

"Not until I know that Doctor Parker is all right," Gage said while gazing over at Cori.

"I can take care of my granddaughter just fine without a Remington hanging around." May balked, then folded her arms across her chest.

"I'm perfectly fine, but I won't be as long as you two keep arguing like this. Can't you both come to some sort of truce?"

"There ain't no truce to come to as long as this woman keeps hoarding all the Zane Grey stuff for herself."

"Look who's talking, you old goat. Your grandson outbid me for the one thing I wanted at this year's conference—Zane's fishing rod. Just because Gage has more money than anyone else at the conference, don't mean he's got to flaunt it."

"I don't want that damn fishing rod. Told him so right after he won the bid. For all I care, you can have it to hide away with all the rest of Zane's things."

"Will you two please stop," Cori said, interrupting whatever her grandmother started to say next. "Let's everybody try to enjoy the day. I'm feeling much better now. No one has to worry or try to take care of me."

"Glad to hear it," Buck said. Then he turned to Gage. "Are you coming, son?"

"If you're sure." Gage's face reflected all the sadness Cori felt over the ongoing battle between their grandparents.

"Thanks, but there's no need for you to stick around. I'm fine. Really."

"Then let's get going, Gage. I got me a list of things I want to see, and we only have a couple hours to get it all in before the train leaves. There ain't no route down this mountain once the last train leaves."

"If you knew anything about Silverton, you'd know there's a bus out of here as well," Gram corrected.

"I know all about the bus, but it's the same as the train. Once the last one leaves around three-thirty there ain't no way to get out of here unless you hitch a ride with someone driving down the mountain."

"No way down, huh?" Gage asked.

"Nope," May affirmed.

It was as if Cori and Gage had the same exact idea at the same exact time, with each of them giving the other a knowing smile.

Chapter Eight

All Gage could think about was finally being able to get Cori alone: no grandparents, no Hailey, and no one around from the conference. They'd each taken off in different directions from the train station. Gage left his gramps at a mine museum for about a half hour with a group of friends while he found the perfect historic hotel. It didn't take long for him to secure a room for the night and to take care of all the details. The woman at the front desk helped him arrange everything. Dinner would be delivered to their room exactly at eight. She assured him that the room was well stocked with water, chocolates and everything Cori needed for a cup of hot tea, along with several different types of juices. He'd made sure the hotel could provide robes, slippers and anything else they might need. He tried not to overlook anything and was counting down the minutes until everyone would get back on that train.

"I'm thinkin' I should catch an earlier bus back down the mountain. This altitude don't seem to be agreeing with me," Gramps said as they stood inside the San Juan County Jail. Gage had been reading about the four small steel cells that sometimes housed as many as six men in canvas hammocks when his grandfather faltered inside one of the cells.

"What's wrong?" Gage asked, as his stomach instantly tightened.

"I'm feelin' all woozy, and that ham sandwich I ate ain't sittin' too easy in my stomach."

"You can't go alone, Gramps," Gage insisted, knowing he would have to abandon his plans for that night. "I'll come with you."

He escorted Buck out of the jail, holding on to him around his waist, thinking this could be more than just altitude sickness. "Maybe we should stop in to see a doctor here in Silverton, first."

"Don't go talkin' about no doctors or callin' no ambulances. I know exactly what I need, and that's to get down off this here mountain. Nine thousand feet is too high for this old dog."

Gage held him close to his side as his gramps leaned into him and let Gage do all the work as they walked. Buck was heavier than Gage had anticipated, and he had to steady himself a few times in order to keep them balanced.

"Gramps, it could be anything. Let me call a doctor, or at the very least I can call Cori. She'll know what's wrong."

Gage hoped his grandfather would agree as he slid the phone out of his pocket and began to unlock it.

"Put that dang thing away. I don't want her messin' around in my business again. I know what I need, and I don't want to hear no more about it or I'll go down by myself." He broke away from Gage, took a few wobbly steps and stopped. Gage ran up and caught him just as he lost his balance and staggered forward.

"What's wrong?" Steve asked, as he and his wife Betsy came up the wooden walkway.

"Not feeling too good," Gramps told him. "Gonna try to catch a bus back down the mountain."

"Where's that Doctor Parker when you need her?" Steve asked.

"Don't need no dang doctor. All's I need is to get me back down closer to sea level."

"We'll go with you," Betsy, offered.

"Thanks, but Gage can take me. You two stay and enjoy yourselves."

"We'll be too worried about you to enjoy it," Betsy told Buck, while gently rubbing his shoulder.

"Thanks, but I know what's wrong with me. Happened a couple times back home in Idaho. I'll be fine, soon as I descend a couple thousand feet. I'll have Gage here call you with an update once we get to the hotel. 'Scuse us, but I wanna get on that there bus before it leaves."

"Here, Gage, take these," Betsy said, handing him a plastic bag. "You two might need some water on the bus. It's a long way down this mountain."

"Thanks," Gage told her, gazing inside the bag to see two bottles of water and a couple protein bars. "But are you sure you won't need these?"

"We won't be hurting for water or food. This town has more than its share of bars and shops. We can easily replenish what we're giving you."

"Thanks," Gage said, glad to have it.

Steve turned to Gage and wagged a slightly crooked finger his way. "You take good care of Buck, or there'll be hell to pay. He's one of my closest friends."

"Yes, sir." Gage replied, thinking how he had no idea

Steve was such a good friend to his gramps. Somehow, he never considered that his gramps had other friends besides the friends he had in Briggs, and even there, most of those people had been closer to his grandma. "I won't let him out of my sight."

"Good idea," Steve told him.

"Do me a favor and take some pictures," Gramps asked Steve. "I been wantin' to see this town for a long time."

"Will do," Steve said, smiling.

"Thanks. Now we best be movin' along."

Betsy gave Buck a hug, and Gage hustled him back to the train station where he'd seen one of those luxury buses standing by. While he bought the tickets, Gramps sat on a bench just outside of the station. As soon as he had his gramps situated on the bus, he'd text Cori to ask her about altitude sickness. He hated that Gramps was so darn stubborn, and decided not to honor his wishes.

He knew Gramps would get all riled up if Cori came on the scene checking for a pulse, so if she would agree to come back with them, they'd have to pretend it was her own doing. Gage knew he had to stop worrying so much about his gramps and give him credit for making it all these years, but even Gramps had admitted that ever since his sweet Rose had passed he wasn't too good at minding his health.

He and Gramps were finally coming to terms with each other, and Gage didn't want to do anything to disrupt their fragile progress. It was too important to him.

Gage didn't know what being alone with his gramps would be like now that they were getting along better, but at the moment all he could focus on was texting Cori about his change of plans. Those "benefits" they both seemed to be counting on would have to wait until his gramps felt better—if that was even possible, with how ornery his grandfather could be.

"I'm sorry," Gramps told Gage as they boarded the luxury bus after Gage had paid for their tickets. As they made their way to their seats, Gage had to fight back the lump that was forming in his throat. He was the one who should be apologizing to his gramps, not the other way around.

When they were seated, Gage said, "Don't ever be sorry for not feeling well, Gramps. It's not something you have any control over. And besides, your not feeling well allows me to take care of you. Payback for all you did for me when I was a kid. I'm sorry I didn't do it sooner. I was too caught up in my own world to think about anything other than what I wanted. I'd forgotten all that you and Grandma had taught me, but I can remember it now that I'm sober again. I love you, Gramps, and there isn't anything I won't do for you.

"Now sit back and relax. We have about an hour and a half until we pull into Durango. You should start feeling better once we begin our descent down the mountain."

"Thanks, son. I'm feelin' better just knowin' I can depend on you."

"Always, Gramps. You can always depend on me," Gage told him as he reached over and squeezed his grandfather's hand.

Gramps grabbed his hand for a moment and then made himself comfortable. Gage wished with all that was in him that his grandfather would allow him to be the grandson he always expected him to be. Gage was ready now, ready to fit into those grandson boots.

CORI, GRAM AND HAILEY had spent the past hour or so shopping at Rocky Mountain Gifts and a couple of other tourist-type stores. They'd grabbed burgers to go at High Noon Hamburgers, and stopped in at the Shady Lady Saloon for sodas. Most of the buildings were the original redbrick structures or had refurbished wooden plank buildings. The town itself had much more of an Old West feel to it than Durango, and Cori fell in love with it. There was even a staged shootout on notorious Blair Street, where most of the saloons and bordellos had once dominated the tiny mining town.

"This has been so much fun," Hailey said as Cori checked her phone for the umpteenth time. Her service had been sporadic at best. So far, there had only been one text from Gage, right when they'd first traded phone numbers. He'd told her that he would be missing the last train off the mountain and hoped she would be doing the same.

She had immediately texted back that she would, but the text hadn't been delivered. Nevertheless, she quickly secured a room for them at the Wyman Hotel and Inn while Gram and Hailey had been trying on a selection of hand-crafted jewelry at one of the shops. She'd sent the clandestine news to Gage, but once again the text hadn't gone through.

"Did you get everything you wanted?" Cori asked her daughter. They stood outside of Natalia's Restaurant on Blair Street.

"Yep, I bought matching T-shirts for Susan and I, and a silver badge for Gage. It's not exactly a hero's medal, but it's close enough."

"I'm sure he'll love it," Cori told her as she checked her phone once again, hoping she'd hit a hotspot soon

so it would start working again. Cori was not about to
get on that train, but now she questioned whether Gage
would actually do the same? If he hadn't received any
of her messages, he wouldn't know she had agreed to
their little scheme.

"Is something wrong, Corina-May? You've been on
that phone most of the time we've been here."

"Sorry, I've been, um, checking on the weather for
our drive home tomorrow."

Hailey looked up at the bright blue sky. "I think it's
going to be another day just like today."

"You can never be too sure. I'd hate to get caught
in a storm."

"Mmm-hmm," Gram said, giving Cori a dubious
look. "Funny that your phone has been working, when
mine hasn't."

They walked in front of a coffee shop and Cori's
phone began to chime, signaling several text messages
had just come through.

Gram's phone also chimed with messages.

"Seems we're back up and running," Gram said as
she reached inside her purse for her flip phone.

Cori grabbed her own phone from her pocket and slid
her finger over the screen until she came to the latest
text message from Gage:

Gramps says he's suffering from altitude sickness. Re-
fuses to let me contact you and won't see a doctor.
Sorry. Change of plans. We're on a bus at the train station headed back to Durango. We leave in 15 minutes.

"I have to go," Cori told Gram and Hailey.

"Go? Go where?" Gram asked, shuffling her many

shopping bags between her two hands. She'd scored big time in Silverton, and Cori felt certain her gram had not only bought several things for herself and Hailey, but that Cori would also be wearing a few new articles of clothing. Gram didn't like to make a big production of her gifts. New clothes simply appeared in Cori's suitcase, neatly folded with the tags removed as if they'd always been there. Gram did the same when Cori and her mom would visit and use the upstairs bedroom. The closet would suddenly contain new T-shirts, dresses, shoes, slacks or any number of things. When Cori or her mom would ask Gram about them, Gram would deny any knowledge, end of discussion.

"Back to Durango. Buck is sick, and he and Gage are taking a bus down the mountain. It's quicker."

"But we haven't even seen everything yet," Hailey protested, her face all scrunched up, looking like a cute little troll.

Cori knew how many events her daughter had given up because Cori couldn't get away from the ER to take her on various school activities, so she certainly didn't want her day cut short because of another emergency Cori had to attend to.

"You guys stay and take the train back as planned. I need to check on Buck. Gage said he won't see a doctor."

Her grandmother frowned. "What makes you so sure he'll talk to you? You know how pig-headed that man can be."

"I know, but if I'm on the bus and his symptoms get worse, I can treat him."

Hailey sighed. "Then you better go, Mom. I like

Buck, and I wouldn't want anything bad to happen to him."

Cori stooped over and gave Hailey a tight hug.

Then she turned to Gram. "Thanks. Love you, guys."

"Just make sure nothing happens to that stubborn goat."

Her grandmother's statement caught Cori by surprise. "I thought you didn't like Buck."

"Whether I do or don't isn't the issue. I'm used to seeing his craggy face at this conference and I'm not ready to hang up our rivalry."

Cori chuckled. "I promise to do everything I can to make sure you two can keep up the contention for many years to come. Now I've got to run if I'm going to catch up with them."

As she rushed for the bus, Cori scolded herself for making such a tenuous promise. Already the self-doubt was creeping in. She had very nearly misdiagnosed a female patient who had come in with what the husband thought was severe anxiety, but because of her own chronic fatigue, Cori had almost overlooked an important factor. The patient had vomited when she first came in. Fortunately, Cori was able to administer the proper treatment in time and prevented any damage to the patient's heart.

That episode had so shaken Cori, that she'd been struggling with that incident ever since.

When the bus came into view, parked perpendicular to the train tracks with its door open as if waiting just for her, she realized what getting on that bus meant: all their plans to be alone that night had to once again be abandoned, and more importantly, she would be diagnosing a problem for Buck that could be life-threatening.

She stopped walking.

GAGE TRIED HIS best to pretend that his insides weren't rattling with fear over his gramps's headache and dizziness. He knew altitude sickness could be fatal if it wasn't treated promptly—something about your heart or your brain retaining water. Neither of which seemed like a good idea for his aging grandfather.

He hadn't heard back from Cori after he'd sent his text. Unlike some of his other messages, he knew this one had been delivered, but what he didn't know was if she would look at her phone in time. He hadn't come right out and asked her to join them on the bus ride back to the hotel, but he'd hoped she would.

If anything serious happened to him, Gage wouldn't be able to recover. Between Cori and his gramps, Gage's nerves were raw.

After last night, he realized just how much he truly cared for Cori. He knew she didn't want a long-term relationship, and for all the right reasons. Neither did Gage, but he could no more ignore his growing feelings for Doctor Cori Parker than he could ignore his grandfather's disappointment in him.

"What's she doing here?" Gramps asked looking straight ahead at the front of the bus. "I told you I don't need no doctor."

Cori's enticing smile lit up her face. "Hey," she said as she approached. "What are you two handsome guys doing on this bus?"

The bus driver closed the door and the coach started to move.

"As if you don't know," Gramps mumbled.

"Am I supposed to know something?" Cori asked, while holding on to the back of the empty seat in front of Gage and his grandfather.

Gage didn't want Gramps to get any more riled up, so he thought he'd put the problem on himself. "I started feeling a little light-headed, so we decided to catch the bus back. And you?"

"Same thing. Nine thousand feet can take its toll on a person if you're not used to it. I knew the bus would get me down the mountain in half the time. How are you doing, Buck?"

"Never felt better."

"That's great, because if you weren't feeling well, you'd tell me, right? Altitude sickness can be dangerous if it's not cared for properly."

"I said I feel great. Ain't no need for either one of you to fret over me."

"We're not fretting, Gramps, we just want to make sure you're comfortable," Gage offered, hoping Gramps would buy the explanation.

"I'm as comfortable as a human being can be while sittin' on a bus. Now you go on and sit with Doctor Parker, so I can stretch out on two seats. No need for you to be babysitting me when there's a pretty girl on this here bus."

"Thanks, Gramps," Gage said. "Would you like some water? A protein bar? Aspirin? I think I have a couple in my pocket. I grabbed a few from your stash this morning."

"That would be perfect for you, Buck. Not that you have anything wrong with you, but sometimes two aspirin will help with any swelling in your body. Not that you have anything going on visibly. I'm just saying, if you did, they would help."

Gage stood up in the aisle, digging the tiny white pills out of his pocket, glad he'd been clear-headed enough that morning to grab them.

"Fine, give 'em to me if it will get the two of you to stop needling me."

Gage handed him the pills along with the bottle of water and one of the protein bars that Steve's wife had given them.

"But you have to take them," Cori insisted.

Buck immediately knocked back the medicine, washing it down with several gulps of water, surprising Gage by being so cooperative. "Do you want to look under my tongue as well?"

"Nope. I trust you," Cori told him then took one of two empty seats in front of them. Moments later, Gage plopped down next to her, looking completely exhausted.

"Thanks," he told her, as soon as hey were settled. "Staying up until two in the morning, debating literary styles and then worrying about—" he rolled his eyes, gesturing back to his grandfather "—is apparently too much for me now that I'm sober. I used to be able to party all night long, go into work the next day and not sleep again until that night without so much as a yawn."

"Sobriety will do that to you."

"Do what?"

"Give you limits. Alcohol does the opposite. You believe you can do almost anything, even though your body and your mind are telling you otherwise."

She slipped off her shoes, pulled her legs up under

her bottom and struggled to get comfy. Gage could tell she was tired as well.

"You sound like you have firsthand knowledge."

She hesitated answering for a moment, as if she was withholding something major. It made Gage uncomfortable.

"Hailey's father was killed in a car accident," she began. "The driver died as well. His girlfriend lived, but is wheelchair-bound for the rest of her life due to a spinal cord injury. She was nineteen at the time. The driver, Daniel Martin, a renowned chef, had been out celebrating the grand opening of his new restaurant. His best friend knew how much he'd been drinking and tried to take his keys but, in the end, couldn't hang on to them. From what the police could piece together, Daniel had twice the legal limit of alcohol in his blood when he decided to pass four cars and a slow-moving motor home on a busy wet road only three blocks from our house. My husband, Jeremy, had just made the right-hand turn onto that street and literally had nowhere to go and no time to get out of the way. Daniel was evidently traveling close to a hundred miles an hour. The two cars disintegrated, and both drivers passed away at the scene. It was a miracle that Daniel's girlfriend survived."

Gage sucked in the breath he'd been holding while she spoke. He'd heard drunk-driving stories over the years and had always told himself he was above all of that. He'd never get behind the wheel drunk, but, God help him, maybe he had on a couple of occasions.

Never had he truly considered the cruelty of the aftermath of an accident like he had while listening to Cori.

"That must have been horrific for you, and everyone

involved. I'm so very sorry." He wanted to say more, but couldn't think of the proper words.

"Thanks. I'm slowly learning how to take my life back. Hailey deserves as much."

She drank from the bottle of water she pulled out of her purse, and rested her head on his shoulder. His heart broke for her, and for Hailey, who lost her daddy before she really had a chance to get to know him.

And all because someone had chosen to abuse alcohol and then drive.

The thought caused him to be disgusted with his past behavior and vow that he would never drink again.

"We should both try to catch some sleep," Cori said. "Buck will be okay now that we're going down the mountain. The aspirin will help him relax. He might even sleep. By the time we get back to Durango he should be as good as new."

Gage stroked her hair as she sighed. "Are you sure this isn't more dangerous than you're making it out to be? He seems pretty shaky."

She shrugged. "I'm not sure of anything. There was a time when I knew exactly what I wanted and how to get it. I used to be confident whenever I diagnosed a patient. Now, ever since I almost messed up due to my own fatigue after working too many hours, I second guess everything, even a common cold.

"Buck's color is good and he isn't any more cranky than normal. It might have just been a combination of a lack of sleep, a lack of real food, the altitude and whatever else is on his mind."

Gage hoped her assessment was correct. Anything more than what she diagnosed and he would never be able to forgive himself for not insisting Gramps see a doctor in Silverton.

"I'd hate for it to be something more dangerous."

"Unless I can give him a real physical I can only go by what's in front of me, but from observing him, he seems fine now."

Gage closed his eyes for a moment and tried to relax. He felt a lot less anxious about Gramps, knowing Cori was on board.

"By the way, not that it matters now but I reserved a room for us in Silverton for tonight," Cori said, shifting in her seat.

Gage could hardly believe what she'd just said about the room. "I did, too, at the Grand Imperial."

She snickered. "The Wyman. I thought it was more masculine."

"The Grand Imperial seemed more feminine. I thought you'd enjoy it."

"Aren't we the couple who likes to please."

He chuckled while he caressed her face, kissing the top of her head. "The best laid plans…"

They sat in silence for a while, watching the lush scenery slip by through the extra-large windows, her head resting on his shoulder, their fingers intertwined.

"I don't think I've ever felt this comfortable with a woman before," he said, stroking her silken hair. "Even with my ex, I always felt compelled to be doing something. We shared very little downtime, and even then, we'd both be working on our laptops or tablets or checking our phones. I always thought being with a woman meant I had to entertain her somehow, and if I couldn't do that, then I worked. But being with you feels totally different, almost as if just being together is enough."

She kissed him, stirring up warm thoughts down deep within him. If this was how she handled friends with benefits, he could only imagine how amazing it would be if she loved him.

She settled back down on his shoulder again, as he stroked her hair and gazed out the window thinking that giving her up was going to be tough.

"Did you have a plan on what we'd say to our families?" Cori asked.

"We wouldn't say anything. We'd simply miss the train and we'd text our grandparents with our apologies."

"My plan exactly."

They fell silent once again, gazing out at the noble mountains and rushing streams that passed by their view. It had been years since Gage had been able to turn off his erratic thoughts and not stress over something he still needed to do. The last time he remembered sitting with nothing to do was on his grandfather's porch. Gage had been around fourteen or fifteen, and he and his gramps had just come in from a morning ride to check on the livestock, something his gramps and his ranch hands did each morning.

He remembered how the two of them had sat on that porch for almost two hours each morning, chatting about the blue sky, the horses in the barn or what they would have for lunch. Most of the time they were silent, Gage rocking in his favorite chair and Gramps comfortable in the wooden chair he'd crafted from an old birch tree he'd chopped down with Gage and his dad.

Those were the times when his grandfather would tell him how much he hoped Gage would one day take over the ranch. How he knew Gage's dad never took to ranching, but that Gage was a natural cowboy who could rope and ride as good as any ranch hand. He remembered how special his gramps had made him feel, and how he wanted to grow up and do just that, take over the ranch…until college and being "successful" and trying to stay successful got in the way.

Now, as Gage reflected on his past and snuggled with Cori, he longed for those days on the ranch, longed to be back with his grandparents. He wished he could introduce Cori and Hailey to his grandma, and show them around the ranch his grandparents loved so much. He knew both Hailey and Cori would love it as much as he did, especially Hailey. He would teach her how to ride, and his gram would have loved to teach her how to make her famous strawberry pie. She would have had such fun with a great-grandchild to dote over like she'd doted over him when he was young. He remembered the sound of his grandmother's raspy laugh, and how they'd sometimes laugh so hard they'd cry. How she loved to be silly with him, and dance around the kitchen. And how loving she was, not only with him, but with everyone she came in contact with. Her kindness and generosity were well-known throughout the Teton Valley. There wasn't a person that Gage had ever met in Briggs who had anything negative to say about Rose Pryde Remington.

The woman was an absolute angel, and it finally dawned on him what a totally self-centered, arrogant jerk he'd become.

He'd missed his own grandmother's funeral, and for what? Because he thought he'd be famous with one appearance on a TV show. He'd been an egocentric idiot.

In the end, his boss had cancelled his trip and Gage never got the opportunity.

"What the heck was I thinking?"

Cori stirred and gazed up at him looking all sleepy eyed. "Are we there?"

He gently slid her hair off her face.

"No. Sorry to wake you. I was thinking about something and got carried away."

She stretched and sat up, putting her feet on the floor.

"What's wrong? You look gloomy. Buck is going to be fine, I promise. Don't worry. I'd tell you if I thought his situation required immediate action."

He forced a grin, but it didn't help his degenerating disposition. She looked so beautiful and innocent against the backdrop of the mountains. He knew he didn't deserve her interest, even if it was for only a short time.

"I'm a real jackass," he said. "You really shouldn't have anything to do with me. I missed my own grandmother's funeral because of a misguided idea that fame was more important. I was such an inconsiderate fool. Maybe I still am, and you should run away from me as soon as possible."

"I'll doubt that, thank you very much." And she stretched up and gently kissed him with all the warmth and compassion he hadn't earned.

"We all do things we regret. It's whether or not we learn from our failures that matters. Have you told your grandfather how sorry you are?"

"Not yet."

"You have time. When you're ready, I'm sure you'll tell him, and when you do, you'll both be better for it."

When she rested on his shoulder again, he could

barely keep his emotions from pouring out. She truly did remind him of his grandmother Rose, exactly like Gramps had said. It was her honest nature and her ability to make him feel decent and whole again.

WHEN THEY ARRIVED back in Durango, Buck seemed to be in good spirits and was feeling a lot better.

"I'm gonna relax in my room for a while, maybe do a little reading," he said as they crowded together in the small elevator inside the Strater Hotel.

"Mind if I join you?" Gage asked. He didn't want to leave him alone.

"You don't need to be worried about me, son. I'm feeling much better."

"It's not that, Gramps. I just thought we could sit and read together like we used to when I was a kid. Compare thoughts on the story. You know, critique Zane's work."

Some of the best times Gage remembered from those summers happened in the evening when everyone would find a book to read, mostly Zane Grey books, and spend a couple hours each night after dinner reading and discussing the stories. They didn't watch TV or disappear into a room to be by themselves. Summer on the ranch was about hard work, riding, family activities, and spending time together, talking, exchanging ideas, telling bad jokes and laughing.

"You want to do that now?" Gramps asked, his eyes watery.

"Yes. Why not? Seems like a good time to read."

"Mind if I join you guys?" Cori asked. "I haven't read a book in I don't know how long. Hailey and my grandmother won't be back for a few more hours."

"If you two are sure this is how you want to spend

your afternoon, then come right on over. I've got me an assortment of books, some I just bought during the auction, some first editions that Gage picked up and some been given to me by friends."

The elevator doors opened and Gramps led the way back to his room.

Once inside, Gage and Cori sorted through the stacks of books on various surfaces in the room, each picking a classic tale. Gage couldn't believe all the books Buck had bought at the auction, many of them first editions with their jackets. He would love to one day have a house with an expansive library that would hold all these books, not only written by Zane Grey but by other famous Western writers like Elmore Leonard, Conrad Richter and Larry McMurty. When he was a kid, Western books and cowboying were all he could think about. Somehow he'd like to get back to those thoughts and dreams.

Gage ordered a couple cheese boards from room service, while Cori walked to the vending machine at the end of the hallway for a few sodas. Once they were settled in, with Cori all comfy on the spare bed, and Gage on a chair with his legs propped up on Cori's bed, each of them having chosen a Zane Grey book to read, Gramps said he had an announcement to make.

"I've been doin' a lot of thinkin' since your grandma passed. Got a lot more time on my hands now that I'm alone in that big ol' house."

"I'll come and visit more, Gramps. And I'll get the rest of the family to do the same," Gage said, looking up from *The Vanishing American*, one of Zane Grey's more controversial books.

"I'm not tellin' you this so's you can fill my house

up with guests. You need to be still for a minute, son, and hear me out."

"Sure, Gramps. Whatever you want."

"I got plenty of friends who stop by to check on me, and the people who work for me give me peace of mind that my animals are in good hands. But running the ranch is a lot of work for one person. I have to admit, when it came to numbers, your grandma knew her stuff. She handled all the money and paperwork that went with it. All I ever did was the physical part, which I'm seein' ain't enough. I gotta face the truth."

"Getting a good accountant to take over the finances isn't a problem, Gramps. I can introduce you to my guy. He's the best," Gage offered thinking he would be more than happy to step in and help out his gramps with whatever he needed.

"Thanks, son, but I don't need your dang accountant. I already got me one of my own. You're not listening to me, son, and you're not letting me get to my point." He took in a deep ragged breath, then quickly let it out. "Here's the point I've been trying to get to. I've made up my mind. I'm selling the ranch."

"Don't kid, Gramps. You would never sell your ranch," Gage said, knowing that his gramps had to be trying to get a rise out of him, testing to see if he would bite. Apparently, his grandfather still wanted to be ornery and cause an argument. Well, Gage refused to participate. He would not let his grandfather rile him up.

He settled lower in the chair, and re-crossed his feet on the bed.

"Already got it on the market. Did it right before I left for this here conference."

Gage sat up instantly, planting his feet firmly on

the carpet. If this were true, he couldn't understand why Buck hadn't mentioned it before. "If it's money you need, Gramps, you know I'll give you whatever it takes."

"Not everything can be solved with money, son. It's time to let it go. I'm not the man I used to be when your grandmother was alive. 'Sides, she liked that there ranch more than I ever did, and she's gone now. It's time I made peace with that fact and moved on."

"To what, Gramps? You don't know anything else but ranching."

Gage knew all about his grandfather's past, how he scrimped and saved to buy his first piece of land, the first few horses, some steer.

"I got me a brand-new fishing pole, thanks to you, and I intend to take up the sport full-time. If Zane could spend all his free time fishing, then by golly, so can I."

"That was a hobby of his, not his life's work. Ranching is in your blood."

"It might be, but I've spilt enough of it over the years trying to keep that place going. I'm done now. Time for someone else to run it. I want to enjoy the time I got left doin' things that make me happy, with people who make me happy."

Gage looked to Cori. "Can you believe this? He's going to let some stranger take over the Circle R ranch."

"It's his property. He can do whatever he wants with it."

Gage knew she meant well, but he sure didn't like how it sounded. "You're not helping."

"Was I supposed to?"

"Yes. You should be on my side."

"I would be if I knew what side you were on."

"The side that convinces him to keep his land. That it belongs in our family. That it's part of my heritage."

"It may be part of your heritage, but you sure got a funny way of showin' that you care one lick about that land," Gramps argued. "You ain't been on it since you were a teenager." He stuck a slip of paper in the book to mark his page, closed the book and placed it on the bed next to him.

Gage looked to Cori for backup, but instead she said, "He has a point."

"Can I help it if school got in the way?" Gage said. "If college and getting straight A's kept me in New York, or getting married and making a good living got in the way of taking a vacation?"

"Is that what you thought those summers were? A vacation?" Gramps sounded incensed, but was somehow managing to control his anger.

Cori slipped out of bed and grabbed her purse. Gage turned to her. "You don't have to leave."

"This is between you and your grandfather. I shouldn't be here."

"Stay," Buck said. "You'll keep my grandson here from making a complete ass out of himself."

"If that's what it takes to make you change your mind, then yes, I'll be more than happy to make an ass out of myself. You don't know what that land means to me. I…" Gage began, but then thought better of it and stopped mid-sentence. He knew how stubborn his grandfather was, and trying to convince him not to sell now that he had obviously made up his mind was about as useful as trying to train a hound dog not to howl.

Gage didn't know why that saying popped into his head, but at the moment, it seemed completely relevant.

"Son, that land is mine to do with as I please, just like the good doctor said. I'm too old and tired to run it on my own anymore, and I ain't waitin' around for you to come to your senses. 'Sides, I got an eye on a sweet little bungalow in town. Got some land around it so's I can plant some vegetables in the summer."

"And that's enough for you? Fishing and some vegetables? After everything you promised me, you're going to sell the ranch and move into a bungalow in town."

"You made it plain and clear you don't want no part of cowboying, just like your dad. He never did take to ranchin'. There ain't nobody left for me to give it to, so I put it on the market, and I hope to have me a couple offers by the time I get back. I hear summer's a good time to sell a ranch of this caliber, some two hundred acres of prime grazing and farming land. The Snake River runs right through it. Ranchers like water runnin' through their land. Should make it easier to sell. Circle R is one of the finest ranches in all of Idaho— it should bring in some mighty good cash. You, of all people, should appreciate that."

"Money's one thing, Gramps, but your ranch is something else." Gage felt as if he'd been sucker punched by his own grandfather. The idea of his grandfather selling the ranch never even occurred to Gage. It wasn't in the realm of possibilities. "You always told me the ranch was mine," Gage said, hoping that clearly stating the facts might change his mind. "You promised me that I could run it one day."

"I did, and it was true as long as I knew you would live there and work it. That's not true anymore, hasn't been for a lot of years. If I gave it to you, you'd just sell it and add the profit to your pile. This way, I can live in comfort off that money and maybe do some good for some deserving people I know. You don't care one bit about the Circle R, at least not the way you used to. It's the idea of it, the memory of those summers, that you get all nostalgic for, not workin' the land or caring for what lives there. I finally faced the truth when my beautiful Rosie passed. She loved you more than anythin'.

"I've forgiven you for your lack of compassion, son. This trip has forced me to see there's still a good part of you that loves your family, and you're tryin' mighty hard to do right by me. That's a good start, but your cowboying days are in your past, and there ain't nothin' I can do to change it. Not anymore."

Gage stood, running a hand through his hair. There was a lot of truth to what Gramps was saying, and Gage knew it. "Gramps, I am so very sorry I missed Grandma's funeral. There was no excuse for it. I was dead wrong, and I know there's nothing I can say to make it up to you. But I'd like to try. Maybe my cowboying days are over, but that doesn't mean we can't find a way to keep the ranch, especially if we work together to find a solution."

"A ranch don't run well with a long-distance solution. 'Sides, I don't want to take the chance you'll lose interest after a bit and I'll end up in the same position I am now. My mind's made up, son."

"Isn't there something I can say to make you change your mind?"

A deep smile creased his grandpa's lips as he glanced at Cori, who smiled right back at him, but Gage could tell this was a dismissive grin. He'd seen it many times before on his gramps whenever he'd had enough discussion on a subject.

"Gage, there ain't nothin' at all you could say. Sayin's just words, and words are only half the truth. It's what's in your heart that counts. What you take the time to do says it louder than if you shouted your feelings from a mountaintop. And so far, how you behave convinces me that I'm doin' exactly what I have to. Now, if you both don't mind, I'm needin' a nap before I meet someone for dinner. I want to be at my best. It's important."

"But we're not through here." Gage balked. He didn't want to give up. Not like this.

Gramps stood, went over to the door and opened it. "Yes, son, we are."

Gage sighed and headed for the door, along with Cori. His heart ached and he blamed himself for his grandfather's decision. There had to be something that would change his grandfather's mind, and Gage was determined to find it.

"Don't forget your books," Gramps said.

"But those are yours," Cori countered.

"I want you both to have them. Consider them my gift to you."

"Thanks, Buck," Cori said, as she grabbed her copy of *Call of the Canyon* off the bed and gave Buck a tight hug and a kiss on his cheek before she left his room.

"This is not over," Gage warned, as he stomped out of the room without his book. There was no way he would allow his grandfather to sell that ranch, not now, not ever.

Chapter Nine

"I didn't know ranching meant that much to you," Cori said as she sipped a cup of first flush Darjeeling tea from a pink teacup. A matching pot sat on the table, along with local honey and a creamer filled with steamed milk. The arrangement was almost perfect, except for the foamy milk. She'd ordered the milk warmed, but apparently the barista didn't quite understand what that meant.

Gage sipped a latte from an oversize mug. They sat inside a bakery down the block from the hotel and shared a plate of some of the best macaroons Cori had ever tasted. She was feeling a bit shaky from both the sugar and her third cup of tea, but she couldn't stop herself from enjoying the fine delicate taste.

"It doesn't, or at least I didn't think it did, but when Gramps said he was selling the place, something snapped. I can't accept his ranch not being in our family anymore, and I can't figure out if what he said is true."

"Which part?"

"All of it, part of it, any of it. That he's really going through with selling the ranch. It doesn't make sense."

He took a sip of the latte and foam stuck to his lip.

"You'd look good in a mustache," she said, snickering.

"What? This is serious."

"Not as long as you have foam on your upper lip, it isn't."

He sat back, chuckled and wiped his mouth with a paper napkin. "That's my problem. I take everything too seriously. I walk around with a continuous chip on my shoulder, and Gramps keeps swiping at it, but I'm holding on with steel gloves." He took in a deep breath and let it out. "I'm a grown man, and Gramps is still teaching me lessons. How can that be?"

"Seniors have a lot to teach us about the intricacies of life. All we have to do is listen."

He leaned forward again. "You believe that, don't you?"

"Never used to, but the more I'm around my grandmother and Buck and everyone else at this conference, I'm coming around to realize all that I've been missing. Every time I'd call my grandmother to see how she was doing, the call ended up being exactly what I needed to hear. I'll never know what she got out of all those calls, but in listening to what she was doing and how she was taking charge of her life after my grandfather died, I gradually learned how to cope with my own grief."

Cori hadn't really thought about it that way before, but now that she put her feelings out there, she could see just how much she benefited from those calls. Without her knowing it consciously, those calls were probably the reason that the first place she'd thought to go to de-stress and figure out what she wanted out of life was her grandmother's house. It all made sense now.

"Your grandmother's a lot different than my grandfather. She's calmer, and sweeter, not the belligerent old man that he's turned into."

Gage seemed restless. He kept moving in his chair, sliding his feet under the table then back out again. She suspected the conversation was hitting a nerve.

"That's all superficial stuff. You heard him today. You saw him. He's vulnerable. Plus he loves you more than he likes to show."

"And you got that from his wanting to sell his ranch out from under our family?"

"Precisely. It's a test, and I'm thinking you failed miserably."

He sat back, cocking an elbow over the back of the chair, a look on his face as if she'd just said something completely preposterous.

"What? That's not true. It can't be, or I'm a complete idiot."

"Absolutely true, at least the way I see it, and I'm pretty good at this kind of stuff."

He leaned forward, taking another sip of his latte, appearing to mull over what Cori had said.

"I don't understand. I told him I didn't want him to sell it. I made that clear, but he kept pushing that he had to get rid of it."

"That's because you never told him why you didn't want him to sell it."

"Yes I did. Well, I tried to."

"Not really. You rattled on about family and his promise to you, but you never once talked about what really kept you away from your grandmother's funeral. I think he deserves to hear that. You apologized for it, but you didn't tell him the facts."

Several teens entered the bakery, and proceeded to the glass case filled with a wide assortment of macaroons. Maple happened to be Cori's favorite, and they were almost out. She wondered if she should hurry and buy a few more before they were all gone.

When she looked back at Gage, his eyes had watered. Obviously, she'd hit a soft spot and hadn't even considered the power of her words. "I'm sorry," she told him. "Sometimes I can come across sharp and to the point. It's a habit I've fallen into during the past year or so. It allowed me to keep my distance with my patients. I know now that was a mistake."

"No need to be sorry. You're absolutely right. I couldn't go back for my grandma's funeral because I knew if I did, I would never have left. My life had turned into a lie, and I'd given up everything I loved for a drink, for that high. I'd lost everything my grandparents had taught me about honesty, and doing the right thing no matter the cost. Gramps stands for hard work and duty. I stand for what's easy and the next party."

"I don't think you can say that about yourself now. You've changed. You stopped drinking. You're here in Durango, attending a conference with your grandfather because you want to mend fences. I can see it in you, hear it in your voice and I like it. I like it a great deal."

"I admire and love him so much that sometimes, when I think of anything happening to him, I can't breathe. That day in the lobby when I saw him lying on the floor, I thought if he didn't make it, well, I don't know what might have happened."

"Have you told Buck any of this?"

He shook his head. "No. I've never said it out loud before. Not even in an AA meeting. Only to you. Here. Now. Thank you."

He reached across the table and took her hand in his, running his thumb over the softness of the palm of her hand. An intense heat sparked across her skin as she gazed into his eyes, causing her to remember his kisses.

"I didn't do anything."

"Yes, you did. You forced me to face the truth and I'll be forever grateful for that."

"But it's not me you should be telling the truth to, it's your grandfather."

He let go of her hand.

"That'll take some courage, and at the moment, I seem to be lacking in that department."

"Take another swig of your coffee. I hear caffeine is a courage builder."

"Since when?"

"Since that's all we have at the moment." She grinned and he instantly lightened up. She loved that she could get him to smile even when the situation seemed dismal.

"I can think of something much more delightful that might help."

He was finally on the right track as a sly smile spread across his face, lighting up his whiskey-colored eyes, and she knew exactly what he was referring to.

Cori feigned being coy. "What's that?"

"Follow me, and all will be revealed."

He finished off his latte, wiped his mouth on a napkin and stood, staring down at her as if there was no one else in the restaurant.

"Is that a promise?"

He reached out for her hand, and she took it without hesitation.

"You bet your sweet..." But she stopped him in mid-sentence with a kiss, thinking that finally nothing was going to get in their way, and she didn't care who knew it.

CORI'S BLOODY NOSE didn't start until they were in the elevator on their way up to Gage's room. As soon as it happened he insisted she not be alone, even though she wanted to change out of her now-bloody clothes.

"I'll come with you," he told her, as she tried not to bleed on him, herself or the floor. She knew she felt a bit shaky, but the nosebleed came as a complete surprise. She hadn't had one since fifth grade, when Tony Cerami accidentally hit her in the nose with his elbow during a rowdy game of tag.

Once the bleeding had slowed to a minor inconvenience, she changed into leggings and a long top, put her hair in a ponytail and followed Gage back to his room, where he made her comfortable on his bed, propping up pillows behind her back so she could lean up against the antique wooden headboard.

He had ordered dinner from room service while she'd changed, and the trays of hot food waited on the small table under the windows while Gage fussed over her. "Are you sure you don't want to eat at the table?"

She was finally comfortable, the bleeding had completely stopped and she really didn't want to move. It had been a taxing day and she was about thirty different kinds of tired.

"Thanks, but I'm not getting out of this bed until I have to."

He lifted an eyebrow. "Is that a promise?"

"Hold your horses, Cowboy. I only meant that I'm still not ready for prime time."

"How you tease."

"You're easily tempted."

"Only when it comes to you."

He picked up the tray that contained noodle soup,

baked salmon, steamed veggies and fries, her comfort food. He brought it over to the bed, then went back for two small bottles of water and placed them on the nightstand next to her.

Then he leaned over and kissed her, igniting the deep passion she felt for him, but she knew she'd be toying with another nose bleed if she took the kiss any further. She needed nourishment, in the worst way, and some rest.

She decided the nosebleed was the direct result of the dry air, the altitude and way too much caffeine. If she counted all of the lattes and cups of tea she'd consumed during the day, she'd had at least six—way too much when your body is trying to adjust to a higher elevation.

Her phone chimed, interrupting the kiss.

"I have to answer this," Cori said, as she pulled away and opened the message. It was a text from Gram: All okay here on train. What about there? She texted back to say everything was fine with Buck.

She showed Gage the text. "Have you noticed anything odd about our grandparents' feud lately?"

He studied the message. "Apart from the name calling and crazy competitiveness, not really."

"Do I detect sarcasm in your voice?"

"Only because your grandmother seems to know the exact moment when we're kissing. And I don't like to be interrupted when my lips are on yours."

"Is this better?" she asked, kissing him again. This time when their tongues touched, Cori could barely control her reaction. She wanted so much more from him than a simple kiss, and she wanted it now.

His hand slipped down to her breasts, gently caressing each one through her shirt. She hadn't worn a bra precisely for this reason. Her senses were heightened and she didn't want him to stop.

But he did, jarring her out of the seduction with a quick withdrawal.

"You should eat something first," he whispered as he moved away from her. "I want to be sure you're okay before we take this any further."

"I'm fine," she told him, lying. When she dabbed at her nose with a tissue, it stained pink. She knew she wasn't completely healed yet, and even felt a bit woozy.

Or was that pure lust for this gorgeous man?

"I can tell you're not being completely honest with me. You look a little pale and I don't think pale is the color of 'fine.' Especially after we just kissed."

She leaned back on the pillows. "Okay, you've got me. I'm still a little shaky, but I don't want to be. We only have a couple hours until my family returns."

"You're staying right here tonight. I'm not letting you go."

"I can't. Hailey will want to tell me all about Silverton and the ride back to Durango. Plus, I don't want her to get the wrong idea. We already agreed to that."

He walked over to the small table, pulled out one of the two chairs, sat down and proceeded to take a bite of his burger.

"What are you doing?" she asked. "There's plenty of room on this bed for you."

"No, there isn't. I can't be that close to you, knowing you don't have anything on under that shirt. It's driving me crazy."

She took a bite of her salmon. "Then you better sit right there while I eat."

"I intend to do just that, but nothing will keep me away when you finish."

"Is that a promise?"

"You have my word as a cowboy."

She took another bite, then another. Each bite of food seemed to restore her strength. "You're a Wall Street trader."

She drank down some of the noodle soup and delighted in the perfectly seasoned broth. It was exactly what she needed…soup and Gage Remington holding her in his arms. The vision caused her to eat faster.

"Not today, darlin'. Today I'm a lost cowboy lookin' for his girl."

"I'm right here, handsome," she told him as she slid the tray to the foot of the bed then slowly removed her shirt.

"Are you sure you're ready for this?" Gage asked as he walked toward the bed, his eyes burning with desire for her.

"I've been ready since the first moment I met you."

He picked up the tray and placed it on the floor, then he removed his shirt and pants. Cori slid down on the bed and watched the muscles in his chest and arms stretch and retract as he slipped out of the rest of his clothes. His chest was everything and more than she had imagined that night on the dance floor. He was magnificent to look at, every muscle defined with a whisper of chest hair.

"Why didn't you tell me sooner?" he asked.

"Timing wasn't right."

"Is it right now?"

She nodded as he crawled on top of her, covering her lips with his, his tongue pressing against hers, one hand caught up in her hair and the other gently caressing her breasts.

She felt vulnerable and in control all at once. Vulnerable because she knew instantly this could never be just sex. This man had captured a part of her heart, and now he was on his way to capturing everything else about her. But she'd made an agreement with him, an agreement that their relationship would end tomorrow.

"Are you feeling okay? We'll take it slow, just in case."

"I wouldn't want you any other way."

"A woman after my own heart," he said in a deep voice, his eyes smoky with passion.

He gently eased her out of her leggings, then he slid her panties off her hips and dragged them slowly down her legs, kissing her hips and legs as he made his way to her feet. He tossed her panties on the floor along with his briefs. Then he slowly made his way back up her legs, dragging kisses along the insides of her calves and thighs until he gently pressed his lips on her sex, then her tummy and the swell of her breasts. She was mad with desire for him.

"And your body," she teased.

"But I thought we were taking this slow and easy."

She ran her fingers over his broad shoulders and down his arms as he kissed her neck and tickled her ear with his tongue. Reason told her she was about to lose herself to this man, and she tried with everything that was in her not to let that happen, but his lovemaking was too real, too raw. With each touch, each kiss, she knew his emotions ran deep. And despite what he'd said about them being friends with benefits, she could tell by looking deep into his eyes that he felt every inch of her in his heart.

She tried to hold back, tried not to give herself to him as he entered her. Somehow he'd slipped on a condom without her noticing and now she was holding back at the last minute.

"Relax," he told her. "I'm here now. I won't hurt you."

She lost herself in his eyes, feeling herself drift into his warmth.

"Wrap your legs around me," he whispered.

She lifted her bottom and slowly did as she was told, opening herself up to him despite her apprehensions. Suddenly all reason slipped from her mind replaced by passion and pure lust. Cori could no longer focus on anything other than the way he felt inside her, her hunger for him all-consuming.

God, why did he have to such a good lover? Why did he have to make her want him more than anything else she'd ever wanted in her entire life?

His movement seemed deliberately slow and methodical, as if he was a bit afraid to move with the rhythm he needed to climax.

"Everything okay?" he asked, confirming her apprehensions.

"Everything's marvelous. You feel so damn good."

"That's all I wanted to hear, kitten. You're amazing. So soft. So warm. So willing."

He kissed her as his rhythm intensified, then he pulled away to stare down at her, causing her to feel a rush so intense and deep that her entire body shuddered from the look in his eyes. He thrust in even deeper until she groaned with pleasure.

"Let it go, baby," he told her, as she dug her fingers into his back and helped push him in even deeper.

She reached up and pulled him down until their lips

met and she devoured his cries of pleasure as they both soared over the cliff together, each letting go of all control until there was nothing left but raw emotion, open to each other more than either one of them had ever been in their entire lives.

HE AWOKE IN DARKNESS, alone in his bed. He had no recollection of Cori leaving, yet by all indications she had. He had hoped she would stay the night, despite her having told him that she would have to leave for her daughter. It saddened him to know that it would be their only time together and she had already left him for her family.

Emotion overtook him and he rolled over on his back to stop it from spilling out like a kid who just broke his favorite toy.

"You're awake," her reassuring voice said from somewhere on the other side of the room.

"You're still here?" he said, wiping the tears from his eyes.

She walked over to him, wearing one of his dress shirts. He wanted to reach up, take it off her, slowly, and then make love all over again.

"I texted my gram and told her I was spending the night with you."

"You told her about us?" He couldn't believe she'd been so honest with her grandmother. Could this mean she had crossed some kind of threshold and was now serious about a relationship with him?

"I decided she deserved the truth, no matter what she thought about it." Cori sat cross legged on the bed, facing him. "And you deserve the truth as well."

He didn't like the sound of her voice, dark and somber. He couldn't handle her telling him how she was going to walk away, not after what they'd just shared.

He slipped his hand under his head so he had a better view of her lovely face. "Lay it on me."

"You remember that night when I literally ran away from you, when you told me you were a recovering alcoholic?"

"Are you going to tell me you're recovering as well? Because if you are, I don't care. We can work on staying sober together or go down in a blaze of glory. It doesn't matter to me. I'm in love with you."

She nearly fell off the bed as she backed away, stood and turned on the light.

"Don't say that."

He sat up. "It's true. I'm in love with you, and God help me, I now know I've never been in love with anyone until I met you."

She picked up her clothes off the floor and started putting them on.

"What are you doing?" he asked, confused over her actions. Why would she leave him in the middle of the night? It made no sense.

"Leaving."

He couldn't let her go. Not like this. Not when he just poured out his feelings.

"Why? I know you want to stay. I know you're in love with me."

"You don't understand. I can't be in love with you, ever."

"Yes you can. It's easy, just follow your heart."

"There's no room in my heart for you or anyone like you."

Her words stung, but he refused to believe them.

He knew she didn't mean what she'd said. She couldn't have, not after what they'd just shared.

"Like you told Hailey, there's plenty of room in your heart for love."

She pulled on her leggings and slipped on one shoe, but then couldn't find the other one and got down on her hands and knees to look around the bed and nightstand.

"No, I can't. I just can't. We had a deal."

She didn't look up. Instead she kept searching.

"I changed my mind." He slipped out of bed and slipped on his briefs.

"Help me find my shoe."

"No. Look at me," he demanded, hoping his stern voice wouldn't scare her away.

She stopped searching the floor for her shoe, sat back on her feet and gazed up at him. He squatted down to her level.

"This is our destiny. What are the odds we'd both be attending this offbeat conference, escorting grandparents who hate each other? No one could predict this. It just happened. For whatever reason, we're supposed to be together."

She shook her head. "It was simply a moment in time, and tomorrow we'll both return to our normal lives."

He reached out for her, grabbing her arms with his hands. "I can't let you go. I love you."

"Stop saying that. Nothing good can come of this."

"You and I are here, together. Nothing else matters."

Her defiance tore at his insides. She had to see the truth, had to admit it to herself. He couldn't understand what was standing in her way. Why she just couldn't admit that despite all her terms and plans, she had fallen in love with him.

"You don't understand," she grumbled.

"You belong to me."

"I need my other shoe," she said. As tears slipped from her eyes, he knew her conviction was breaking down, that he was winning the argument.

"You need me."

He wiped the tears off her cheeks with his thumbs, as he gently cupped her face in his hands.

"I need my shoe, damn it. I won't do this. I won't."

He spotted her shoe under the table in front of the window, slowly stood and retrieved it, then handed it to her.

"Just tell me why you're turning me down when I know you love me. I felt it when you gave yourself to me."

Her tears increased as she took the shoe from him and slipped it on her foot. He didn't want to believe she didn't feel something. Her feelings had been right there, open to him, raw and unhampered.

No way did she not love him.

"Because you're…because my…"

She sighed and he knew he'd won the battle, at least for now.

He reached out for her. "Come back to bed. You don't have to go anywhere. Stay with me. Sleep with me. I'm not asking you to love me, but let me love you one more time. Then I'll drive away and you never have to see or think about me ever again."

She hesitated as tears streamed down her cheeks. She was holding something back, something dark that she wasn't ready to free. He hoped his love might change her mind, and she'd tell him the terrible secret she'd been hiding.

"Come on," he repeated, still reaching for her. "Come back to bed."

"I…"

"Don't go. Not like this. Not tonight. Whatever is bothering you, we can fix. I promise."

She sniffled and relaxed into him. He gently touched the tips of her fingers and then reached out for her other hand, spreading out her fingers with his. They touched palms and he drew her in close. A moment later he led her back to his bed, turned out the light and slipped into bed next to her.

He unbuttoned her shirt, taking his time with each button and kissing her warm skin as her shirt fell open. When he folded it back, moonlight washed over her skin, and he couldn't take his eyes off her lovely body. He wanted to remember this moment forever, so instead of kissing her he ran his hands over her body with the tips of his fingers, gently caressing her full breasts and her taut stomach, and then he removed her leggings. This time, he took his time examining the intimacies of her lovely body, lingering between her legs until she moaned with pleasure.

When he finally entered her, he slowed it way down, wanting to feel her body tight around him. Not wanting to rush, he moved easily and steadily with a rhythm that brought them both to tears.

Afterward, he rolled onto his side, and he held her close, burying his face in her fragrant hair until her breathing deepened and he knew she'd fallen asleep. If this was going to be their last night together, he didn't want to be the one who fell asleep first. He wanted to be the one who remembered every detail and nuance of the night, including when dawn broke over the majestic Colorado Mountains.

Then and only then would he release her from his life.

Chapter Ten

Cori snuck out of Gage's room early in the morning, hoping not to wake him and that no one would see her in the hallway. She wasn't in the mood for Steve Court or anyone else from the conference.

When she entered her room, both her grandmother and Hailey were fast asleep. She quickly went into the bathroom, washed up and changed into jeans, a T-shirt and her boots. Then she grabbed her purse, snuck downstairs to the restaurant and hid in a deep booth with a glossy oak table, next to the entrance. The booths were angled in such a way that no one who entered the restaurant could see her unless they stepped in closer and gazed over the top of the dark wooden walls.

She was confused about last night, about her feelings for Gage and what reason told her would certainly happen if she relented to his love for her. God help her, she'd fallen in love with him, but she had to think of Hailey, of their life with a man who could turn back to alcohol on a dime. She felt as though she was betraying Hailey's dad, a man she had loved deeply. A man she thought she would grow old with, until his life was eradicated by another man who was well past the legal definition of intoxication and decided to do ninety on the wrong side of the road.

She knew she had to tell Gage the truth. He deserved that much, but she simply didn't know how.

"Can I get you some coffee?" the cheerful young waitress asked, shattering Cori's thoughts. She wore oversize brown horn-rimmed glasses and her curly auburn-colored hair was pulled back off her face with clips. Her innocent face was scrubbed clean with very little makeup and she was dressed in the same black blouse and black slacks all the waitstaff wore at the hotel. She couldn't have been more than twenty years old.

"Tea, please. English Breakfast, if you have it, or Irish Breakfast will do. Just not Earl Grey. I really don't like Earl Grey. With warmed milk and some honey, if possible." Cori wished that for once a waitperson would listen to her order and bring her exactly what she asked for. She noticed a name tag pinned to the young woman's uniform: Audrey.

"Will you be having the buffet this morning?"

"Yes, Audrey, thank you," Cori answered, retrieving the free buffet ticket the conference had provided from her purse.

Audrey left and returned within minutes with a white ceramic pot filled with hot water, a white mug also filled with hot water, an assortment of tea bags on a doily-clad plate, a small metal creamer of warmed milk and an unopened squeeze bottle of honey.

The young woman was a saint—not an Earl Grey teabag to be found, and everything else was perfectly presented.

"Thank you so much. This is lovely," Cori told her as she tore open the wrapper on the Organic Irish

Breakfast tea and immersed it in the mug of hot water. She watched as the water began to turn a lovely deep amber, and marveled at how this friendly young woman had brought her exactly what she'd asked for. A true rarity. Most of the time the water was tepid, the assortment of tea consisted of one horrible commercial black tea and the rest were herbal, the milk was cold and honey was either nonexistent or the bottle was industrial sized.

Audrey had no idea how badly Cori needed her proficiency this morning.

"So, how are you doing this morning?" Audrey asked, grinning.

Without even realizing it, Cori's eyes watered. "I'm terrible, actually. I'm in love with a man who will probably break my heart and I don't know what to do about it."

The words came pouring out as if she had no control over them, as if someone else had taken over and spilled her heart out on the table for her.

Audrey slipped into the booth next to Cori, and put her arm around her shoulders. "Life sucks, sometimes, especially when we don't know which way to go."

Audrey quickly unrolled the silverware from its black napkin and handed the napkin to Cori. Cori made the effort to dry her tears.

"You are so right. I guess this is one of those times."

"Like my mother says, life is not fair." Audrey shook her head as if this fact was a real shame and something we all had to learn.

"Your mother is a smart woman."

"I didn't used to think so, but now that I'm older I'm finding that she really knows a lot."

"That's what happens when we grow up. We realize

our parents, or in my case, my grandmother, know a lot more than we ever gave them credit for."

"You sound as if you know a lot, as well. You're just not giving yourself enough credit. I do that all the time, and it really sucks big-time when I second guess myself. I usually end up in a stupid situation."

"Me, too."

"See? We both agree. Okay, so what I'm hearing is you said he'll *probably* break your heart, right?"

Cori sucked in a sob. The young woman was making a lot of sense.

"Yes, and I don't know how to handle that."

"The way I look at it, *probably* isn't a for sure kind of thing. *Probably* means he might, not he will. You should have a little faith that he won't ever break your heart. Your chances either way are about the same. Isn't it always better to go with a positive rather than a negative?"

"Yes, always better, but I haven't been completely honest with him."

She shook her head. "See, now, that's a problem. Why not?"

"Because if I tell him the reason why I'm having such a hard time trusting him, it'll put a barrier up between us."

Audrey pulled away, and was silent for a moment. Then after thinking about it she said, "My mom always told me, 'the truth shall set you free.' I think this is one of those times when you need to free yourself. That is, of course, assuming you didn't do something that might land you in prison."

"It's nothing illegal."

"Good, then go for it, babe. It's the best advice I can

give you." Then she giggled. "That's if you want advice from your nineteen-year-old waitress."

"Audrey, you don't know how much your encouragement means to me, especially this morning," Cori told Audrey as she slid out of the booth.

"Then my job here is done. Just let me know when you need more hot water."

"Thanks. I will."

Audrey nodded and disappeared around the corner, to wait on other tables. The restaurant was beginning to get busy as more and more people arrived. Cori couldn't see any faces, just the very tops of their heads.

She knew what she had to do now, knew that Audrey, in her sweet, innocent way, had been right. Nothing in life, other than death, was a certainty, and she'd been acting as if she knew exactly what Gage would do. She'd been using statistics to guide her heart, when she knew better than that.

If the medical profession had taught her anything it was that statistics sometimes had little bearing on a patient's outcome. Some of the most fragile people had made it through intense trauma when by all accounts they should have died, whereas some of the strongest, most healthy people who had been expected to pull through had taken a turn for the worse.

Cori breathed in and out deeply, slowly, and methodically prepared her tea as if it had been a lifelong ritual, pouring in just the right amount of milk and adding the honey, followed by that first sip to be sure the taste was perfect…which it was. And just as she sat back in her private booth, contemplating how she would tell Gage the truth about all her apprehensions, she heard an approaching siren and instinctively knew it was headed straight for the Strater Hotel.

"HE DIDN'T MEET me in the lobby for breakfast and when he didn't answer his phone I knew something wasn't right," Steve said, as Buck was loaded into the back of the ambulance on a gurney. Apparently, Buck had fallen sometime during the night and wasn't able to get up to reach his phone on the nightstand—a dangerous situation for a man of his years. Cori knew his immobility could mean any number of possible life-threatening conditions, the biggest concern being a ruptured spleen or an unstable femoral fracture. She'd given him a brief examination before the ambulance arrived and concluded it was a stable femoral fracture, which could be fixed with pins.

Obviously, they'd do an X-ray and an MRI at the hospital to be sure, but Cori felt certain she had diagnosed him correctly and had warned the EMTs accordingly.

"I shouldn't have allowed him out of my sight," Gage said as Cori tried to assuage his guilt.

"It was an accident. He could have fallen whether you were with him or not," Cori told him. She watched the same two EMTs who had taken Buck to the hospital the first time he fell get ready to close the back doors on the ambulance.

"These things happen to older folks," Steve added. "It's not like I haven't had my share of falls. But so far, thank God, I haven't broken anything."

"But he wouldn't have been on the floor all night without treatment if I'd been there."

"Nobody wants a babysitter, at least not while we're still active," Steve said, patting Gage's shoulder.

"If something bad happens to him, I'll never forgive myself." Gage wore a look of anxiety on his face—not a state he needed to be in at the moment. Buck's condition required a cool head to be in charge, someone who could handle all the paperwork and possible procedures the hospital staff would be throwing his way.

"Buck is getting older, and his agility isn't what it used to be, but he's awake and feisty as ever," Cori said. "He knows what he wants and will probably give the nurses and doctors heck at the hospital."

"I came on this trip to repair my relationship with my grandfather and instead I let him down once again." Gage shook his head. "He's right about me."

"Gage, you're…"

But he was no longer listening. Instead, he'd walked off as the taller male EMT slipped an oxygen mask over Buck's face and the other EMT closed and secured the ambulance doors. Cori watched as the ambulance drove away, lights swirling and sirens blaring, and Gage walked up the street alone. She didn't know where he was going exactly, but Wine and Fine Spirits was located in the direction he was headed.

She wanted to give him the benefit of the doubt, to believe he simply needed some time alone. That he didn't go along with his grandfather in the ambulance because he wanted to drive himself to the hospital so he'd have access to his car, but she also knew this was the perfect time for Gage to cave and give into his craving for alcohol.

Plus, the hotel parking lot was located in the opposite direction.

She walked back inside through the side door of the

hotel with Steve Court by her side. This time she welcomed his presence.

"He's a tough old bird. He'll get through the physical part of this, I'm sure of it," Steve said. "Having his grandson with him will help. But ever since he lost his Rosie, he's been drifting. A woman can handle losing her man, but most men can't handle losing their woman. Something in our DNA. We're not cut out to be alone in our golden years. We don't know what to do with ourselves, and most of the time we don't give a damn without that special lady by our side. Our kids and friends fill in some of the gaps, but for the most part, unless we have somebody who knows how we like our morning toast prepared, our lives can be pretty miserable. Those doctors can fix Buck's body, but it's his heart that needs fixing."

Cori thought about her grandmother and how, despite how much Gram missed Grandpa, she still managed to lead a full life. Steve was right about that much…

Or did she?

Gram's shopping and spending seemed excessive at times. Cori's grandfather had always been the money manager and kept them from overspending. Was her grandmother really managing her grief and loneliness or was she suffering as much as Buck, and Cori was blind to it?

Cori turned to Steve and gave him a hug. "In just five minutes, you've managed to teach me more about aging than I've learned in all my combined years of education and practice. Thank you. Truly, thank you."

When she pulled away from him, his face flushed with what she could only guess was embarrassment. "Anything I can do to help."

"You have no idea," Cori said, and rushed up the two

flights of stairs to her room. She wanted to be at the hospital when the doctors made the diagnosis.

She burst into her room just as her grandmother walked out of the bathroom, dressed and ready for the day. Cori noticed that most of their luggage was neatly stacked by the door.

"We won't be leaving today. Buck fell during the night and I'm sure he has a fractured hip. I just don't know the severity of the fracture. That will be determined with an X-ray or scan. He went off to the hospital about ten minutes ago, and I want to be there with him."

"I heard the siren," Grandma May said. "I somehow knew it was for Buck."

Gram took a seat on the wicker desk chair.

"I'm sorry about Buck. When will we know how bad he is?" Hailey asked while sitting on the bed, still wearing her pajamas.

"It shouldn't take more than a couple hours."

"Will he be able to ride a horse again?" Grandma May asked as she sipped coffee from a paper cup. Cori could tell she was hiding real concern behind her calm voice.

"I don't know, Gram. It depends on how bad this is, and how determined Buck is to recover."

"Is he going to be all right, Momma? He always makes me laugh, and he tells me stories about his ranch in Idaho. He told me we could come visit him whenever we want to and I told him we would. He's so nice. He's not going to die, is he Momma?"

Cori walked over to Hailey and gave her a hug. "He's going to be fine, sweetheart. He just took a tumble, which can happen to anyone. The doctors at the hospital will take good care of him. Whatever's wrong, they'll fix it, I promise."

"Will you be able to keep your promise this time, Momma?"

Cori was busy changing into a pair of black dress pants, heels, a new orange silk blouse and a new white fitted jacket. She didn't want to go to the hospital looking like anything other than a professional, and fortunately her gram had provided her with the clothes to achieve that look.

"What do you mean, baby? I always keep my promises, or at least I try to."

She buttoned up the blouse and sat on her daughter's bed. This was one of those moments when her daughter needed her full attention. Cori prided herself on keeping a promise to her daughter, at least she thought she had.

"You promised that Grandpa would be okay and he died."

Cori caught the look of anguish in her grandmother's eyes. She didn't remember making that promise to her daughter, but if Hailey said she had, then it must be true.

"That was different, honey. Grandpa had been sick for a really long time."

"I know, but you still promised."

Cori reached out and Hailey crawled over and sat on her mother's lap, resting her head on Cori's shoulder. Cori wrapped her arms around her little girl. She smelled of sleep, and was still warm from being under the covers. Cori's baby was growing up at a rapid pace and almost didn't fit in her lap anymore.

Suddenly, she remembered the promise she'd made to her daughter about Grandpa. She'd been working long days to compensate for the time she spent away, flying back and forth to Denver every week to be with her grandparents. She hadn't had time to spend with Hailey, and when she did get a few moments all Hailey wanted to talk about was her great-grandpa. Cori had suspected for quite some time that he wouldn't recover from the cancer that was gaining ground inside his body, but she hadn't had the heart to tell Hailey, so she promised that he would get better without giving it another thought.

A mistake on her part.

"You're right, sweetheart. I did. Sometimes, when I make a promise to you about someone getting better, I'm hoping with all my heart that's what will happen but I don't always know for sure. Would you like it better if I didn't make you a promise I'm not sure about?"

Hailey thought about it for a moment. "I think that would be better, yes. That way, I won't get disappointed when that person doesn't get better."

"I can do that."

"So, is it true about Buck? Will he really get better, Momma?"

Cori's first instinct was to tell Hailey that he would. She had always wanted to spare her child of any undue pain. But Hailey was growing up now, and deserved to know the truth about the people she cared about.

"I honestly don't know, baby. He has a long road ahead of him, but if he works really hard, and takes good care of himself, there's a good chance he'll recover in a few months."

"Should I pray for him, Momma? Do you think that will help?"

"Yes, sweetheart, pray really hard. And pray for Gage as well. This is a difficult time for both the Remingtons."

"I'll pray, too," Grandma May said, as she came

over and sat next to Cori and Hailey, wrapping her arms tight around them both.

GAGE WAS AT his wits' end. He felt that everything he'd said or done in the past few years had led him to this cataclysmic moment. He'd wanted to do right by his grandfather, wanted to mend fences, but instead those fences couldn't be in more disrepair. And if his grandfather didn't make it through whatever malady had sent him off to the hospital, Gage would surely pass away right along with him.

As he headed up the sidewalk, he knew he should be aiming for his car so he could meet his grandfather at the hospital, but Gramps had told him in no uncertain terms to keep his distance. That he didn't need Gage hanging around as if he were senile, that he was perfectly capable of making his own decisions.

Gage had tried to argue his stubbornness away, but he could tell that it only served to agitate Gramps, making it more difficult for the EMTs to treat him. In the end, Gage let it go and tried instead to get his grandfather to calm down, which seemed impossible.

Gage didn't know why his grandfather was insisting he stay away, but he decided to honor his wishes and keep his distance, at least for the initial diagnosis at the hospital. Cori would be there, and that was good enough for him.

Until then, Gage had something he wanted to do and was in no mood for anyone to try to stop him, including Doctor Parker.

As he approached Wine and Fine Sprits, he lingered in front of the shop, the open door taunting him, beckoning him to enter. All he had to do was take the first step. Everything else would be easy and he knew he'd feel so much better once he gave into its pull.

The one problem with relenting happened to be the fact that those evenings at the bar, laughing with his friends, never even came close to the euphoria he felt wrapped in Cori's arms or sitting on a train next to his grandfather or saving Hailey. No amount of whiskey could replace those moments, nor did he want to ever believe it could.

He believed in Gramps, in his ranch, in cowboying and in his love for Cori Parker. He didn't know if any of those beliefs could ever be his to share on a daily basis, nor did he know exactly how difficult it might be to try to make that happen. He only knew they were what made him feel whole again, as if his life had purpose, meaning.

He didn't move for a full minute, remembering how powerful and relaxed he felt with each glass of wine or shot of bourbon. He remembered a scene from a movie with Jimmy Stewart, and how his character described a shot of whiskey as a slap on the back. Gage needed a strong slap on the back right about now. In all honesty, he needed several slaps on the back in order for him to escape all the guilt and fear he was feeling. He wanted nothing more than to be in one of his favorite bars in Manhattan with his friends surrounding him, getting progressively more and more inebriated, laughing about the ups and downs of the market, allowing himself to sink into that hole he would get into and never leave.

Life got a heck of a lot easier after several slaps on the back.

"Can I help you?" the woman behind the counter asked once Gage stepped inside the shop.

Chapter Eleven

Buck's hip surgery was a complete success. Cori's initial diagnosis of a stable fracture of the femoral neck had been correct, and because she'd told the EMTs, the ER staff was able to give him the proper care from the time of his arrival.

Now, as Buck rested in the private recovery room, Cori wondered if Gage would ever make an appearance. So far he'd been completely absent and never responded to any of the text messages she'd sent.

Her instincts told her he had probably stopped in that liquor store and was busy getting wasted somewhere, but her heart wanted to believe he'd been caught up in something far less reprehensible.

In the meantime, only Cori and her gram were allowed in the recovery room at one time. The amazing thing about it had to be her grandmother's reaction to seeing Buck flat on his back hooked up to various machines.

She cried.

"Gram, he's going to be fine. It'll take a lot of physical therapy, but he'll be all right with the proper care," Cori told her as Gram walked to Buck's beside.

Before Gram could answer, Buck held up a wobbly hand and to Cori's amazement, May took it.

"That was some scare, my pet," Gram said as she gazed down at Buck, who couldn't seem to take his eyes off her.

At first, Cori thought she hadn't heard her grandmother correctly. Why would someone who supposedly had a rivalry going with Buck Remington suddenly refer to him as "my pet"?

She couldn't have heard her correctly.

"They say I'm going to be fine, darlin'," he answered, his voice soft and weak from the trauma of the surgery.

Cori didn't want to break up this loving moment, but she had to know what happened to cause them to be so sweet to each other.

"Okay, what's going on? Did I miss something? Since when did you two get to be so…loving?" Cori didn't care which one answered. She just needed an answer, now.

"Since Buck asked me to marry him."

"What?" Cori asked, feeling her knees buckle. She couldn't have heard that correctly. Boisterous Buck Remington had asked feisty May Merriweather to marry him?

"Sit down, dear, you look as a bit peaked," Gram cajoled.

Cori did as she was told and plopped down on a plastic chair at the foot of the bed. "You want to tell me a few more details, Gram? When did this happen? Better still, how did this happen? And are you?"

"Yes, Corina-May, I am. I don't think I have to tell you how, but our love affair began right after Gage bought the fishing rod out from under me. Buck and I were both so angry at Gage that we forgot to be angry at each other."

"Love affair?"

"Yes, dear. Our love affair. We can hardly keep our hands off each other."

"Thank you, but I don't want to know."

"She's a spitfire, if I ever knew one," Buck said, hardly able to speak or stay awake. "Can't let a woman like that get away from me. Life is too dang short."

"But Grandpa hasn't been…" Cori stopped herself from going any further, but the fact remained. Her grandpa had only been gone for less than a year.

"I know, darling, but he wouldn't want me to be alone, and when Buck and I started talking, we realized just how much we had in common. When you get to be our age, you don't know what the next day can bring."

"Or the next night," Buck said, interrupting May's explanation.

"Right," May said, agreeing with Buck. "So we decided to act fast."

"Not fast enough," Buck said as his eyes closed and he fell asleep.

Gram walked over and sat down next to Cori.

"You and Buck are getting married?" Cori asked as her grandmother made herself comfortable on the only other chair in the room.

"Yes," she said and reached over and took Cori's hand in hers. At once Cori felt warm and safe, a learned reaction from years of trusting her grandmother.

"When?"

"As soon as we can get a license. Of course, now that he's had this little misstep, so to speak, we may have to postpone it for a few weeks."

"A few weeks? Buck won't be ambulatory for a couple months, and even that will take a lot of intense physical therapy."

"That's okay. He's going to need me to help him through this time. If I left him alone at a time like this, he might never recover."

Her eyes were clear and calm, as if she knew exactly what she wanted and how to get it. Not a smidgeon of self-doubt.

"Gram, do you know what you're getting yourself into? He may not recover."

"Sweetheart, I love you dearly, but you sometimes dwell on the negative instead of the positive. Yes, I know he may not recover. That's a given. However, with my help, he may recover sooner and be riding again in six months."

Cori knew the odds of that happening were slim to impossible.

"Gram, that's wishful thinking."

"When I was a young girl, growing up in horrible poverty in the Midwest, the only thing that got me through each day was wishful thinking. I couldn't have survived the loneliness of farm living without wishes and hopes and dreams. A lot of my wishes came true, my daughter, you and Hailey being some of them, and of course your dear, sweet grandpa. When you were a little girl, you and I would wish for a hundred things before breakfast. You ought to try it again sometime. You might find that wishes really do come true."

Cori knew she couldn't win the argument, and was in no mood to try. Not when her grandmother was being so unreasonable. She only hoped that wherever Gage might be hiding, he'd surface, completely sober and ready to deal with this new situation.

GAGE STROLLED INTO Mountain View Hospital knowing he'd made the right decision for everyone concerned. He only hoped his grandfather felt the same way.

He'd kept up on his grandfather's progress with updates from Steve Court. The man turned out to be a great friend to both Gramps and to Gage—something Gage never would have guessed from his initial reaction to him.

Now as he stepped off the elevator and headed to his grandfather's room, he felt confident, almost buoyant, that he had the entire situation under control, a trait he admired about himself. No matter what went on around him, if the situation warranted immediate attention, Gage could always take a look at the problem, make a calculated decision and act on it accordingly, at least when he was sober. And right now, he was stone sober.

This moment in time had demanded that he step up and take action, and he'd come through with flying colors. Now all he wanted was for everyone else to go along with his ideas.

He'd picked up some flowers and a vase at a nearby florist and held them in one hand as he pushed open the door to his grandfather's room with the other. He wasn't particularly surprised to see Cori in the room, but May?

"Wow, this is a surprise. I never expected to see you here, May. How's the 'old goat' doing?"

"He just fell asleep. He's doing really well," Cori told him, taking the flowers and placing them on a shelf near the TV.

"Are you okay?" Cori asked, seemingly studying his face.

"I'm fine, why?"

Then she walked in closer, as if smelling his breath. He instantly caught on. She was checking to see if he'd been drinking.

"I'm as sober as a judge, although I've seen my share of inebriated judges. And if you're wondering if I had anything to drink, the answer is no, I have not."

"You have not?"

He shook his head. "Not a drop."

"Then why are you so happy?"

"I'll tell you, but first I want to know how Gramps is really doing. Don't sugarcoat it. Give it to me straight. I called the hospital and a nurse told me that he's doing fine, but that was all she would say."

"Please don't call your grandfather an 'old goat.' He's a wonderful man who needs our positive thoughts and prayers," May grumbled.

Gage looked to Cori for some answers, while heading her way. May had referred to his grandfather as a lot of things, but a *wonderful man* had never been one of them.

"Who is this person, and what happened to your grandmother?" he whispered as he walked in closer.

"Gage," Cori began, "since your grandfather is indisposed at the moment, my grandmother has something important to tell you."

Cori turned to her grandmother, offering her the floor.

"It can wait until Buck is awake again," Gram countered. "I don't want to take away the satisfaction he might be counting on when he tells Gage the big news."

"I don't think it can wait," Cori insisted.

"There's big news? Is this good big news, or is Gramps in worst shape than I've been told?"

"Buck came through the surgery like a champ. Aside from a fractured femoral bone, the man is in amazing shape. The doctors can't believe how agile he is," Cori assured him.

"Then what is it?" Gage demanded.

"It's nothing really. Just a little change in plans," May offered.

"What kind of change in plans?" Gage wanted to know. Cori caught a look of concern on his face.

May shrugged. "It's just that Buck and I will be getting married as soon as possible."

"What?" Gage said as Cori slid the chair she'd been sitting on closer to him.

"Have a seat. It helps," Cori told him.

Gage plopped down in the chair as if his limbs were made out of rubber.

"Married? Why?"

"Because we're in love," May said while smiling down at Buck, who looked completely peaceful.

"At your age?" And as soon as he said it, he realized he'd made a terrible mistake. The old Gage would have thought that, not the new Gage, who didn't drink anymore and had a new respect for the elderly.

"What?" May began, looking as if she would bite off his head if she could. "You think a person can't fall in love in their seventies?"

"Of course they can, but I thought you two hated each other?"

"Hate? Now there's a nasty word. No, no, I didn't like him. But even then, I never *completely* disliked Buck.

I simply didn't like how he would buy up all the Zane Grey memorabilia and then we'd never see it again. Of course, he didn't like that about me either. Now that we're getting married we can share everything. That includes all our Zane Grey loot, and believe me, I've collected more than he realizes over the years."

"I'm sure he has, too, but…have you decided where you'll live?"

"We haven't made the final decision yet. His ranch is on the market and my house is too small."

"May I make a suggestion?" Gage asked. In truth, he thought their love nuptials would fit perfectly into his plan.

"Certainly, but this matter is between your grandfather and me. You two have nothing to do with it." He caught the fire in her eyes and knew he had to tread lightly.

"Well, that's not exactly true," Gage said.

"Yes it is. We're old enough to make up our own minds, thank you very much."

With May being just as ornery as his grandfather, married life between the two of them was beginning to take on a whole new meaning.

"You certainly are, but I just bought my grandfather's ranch. That may have a slight impact on your decision."

Cori moved another chair under her grandmother. She plopped down into it. "But that's not possible. Buck would have to agree, and he would never allow it. He wants it to go to someone who will work it. Matter of fact, we did discuss keeping it for a few more years and working it ourselves. I love ranching. Farming, not so much, but ranching is exciting."

"You can't buy that ranch unless your grandfather

accepts your offer," Cori said, a look of total disbelief on her face.

"Gramps left that decision up to his attorney. I offered a price he couldn't refuse, and he accepted while Gramps was in surgery. I know Gramps may still fight me on this, but I'll argue my position until my last breath. That ranch means too much to me, to Gramps, and now that I know you like ranching, it'll mean too much to you, as well. I did what I thought was right, what I think Gramps secretly wanted me to do but wouldn't say out loud. I had to figure it all out on my own. The paperwork is being drawn up as we speak."

"Now we'll have to move to my place, and I don't want to live there anymore. Way too small. Cori and Hailey can hardly fit in the guest room." May said.

"Then don't. You and Gramps can live on the ranch like you planned."

"He told me if you ever got your hands on it, you'd sell it. Why the change of heart?" May wanted to know.

"Because I found that my heart is the only part of me that knows what I need, and I need that ranch. It's who I am, who I've always been—a cowboy."

"DID YOU MEAN what you said about your being a cowboy?" Cori asked, as she and Gage walked into the Strater Hotel. It had been a taxing day, and Cori was wiped out. All she wanted was to slip into bed next to her daughter and sleep until noon. "I mean, you weren't making that up for my grandmother's benefit, were you?"

"I gave my landlord notice on my apartment this morning. I'm not going back. Aside from some personal things, which my ex-wife can have, and some clothes, which I won't need anymore, there's nothing back there for me."

"So you're moving to…where is the ranch again?"

"Briggs, Idaho. It's in the Teton Valley. A beautiful little town. You and Hailey would love it. I could teach her how to ride. Who knows, maybe she'll grow up and become a rodeo star."

"Instead of a fashion designer? That's her latest ambition, but cowgirl was right up there on the list."

"She can design fashion for cowgirls, or some such thing. I really want you to come out. I know you'll both love it."

It was all happening too fast. Her grandmother was leaving tomorrow on a private air ambulance that Gage had hired. He was moving his grandfather to Teton Valley Hospital so he'd be closer to home.

"What are you saying?" Cori asked him, concerned over the speed with which her life and that of her grandmother's were changing. She had left New York and her job at the ER for something new, but she'd never thought that "something new" would include another man.

"I'm asking you to move to Briggs. Or at least come back with us tomorrow and check it out. You don't have to stay with me, unless you want to."

"I have to think of Hailey," Cori told him. "I can't run off with a man I've only known for a few days."

"I understand, but at least come for a couple weeks. It's a big ranch house. I don't know what kind of shape it's in, but there are at least five or six bedrooms."

"Hailey's just getting used to her grandmother's house. How am I supposed to move her again?"

"You told me that was only temporary. A place for you to rest until you decided what to do. Well, you look rested to me. Why not decide what to do while in Briggs? It's a great town. Hailey will make friends in no time."

Gage pushed the button for the elevator, the door opened and they stepped inside. Cori kept her distance and her arms crossed over her chest. When the elevator stopped, they got out and walked through the hallway until Gage stopped in front of a door. That's when Cori realized they weren't on her floor.

"This is your room. My room is on the second floor. Hailey's waiting for me."

"This could be our last night together. I want you in my bed, where you belong. You've got the rest of your life to sleep with your daughter, or whomever you choose, but tonight you're mine."

"But I haven't decided anything yet. I should talk this over with my grandmother, with Hailey. I can't..."

He smiled and stepped closer to her. She could feel the heat swirling through her body. She wanted him now more than ever.

"You can't what?" he asked, his lips only a hesitation away from hers.

"I can't love you. You're all wrong for me, despite what Audrey says."

"Who's Audrey and why do I like what she says?"

"She's a waitress in the restaurant downstairs." He kissed her neck and slowly ran his lips up to her chin making her knees weak and her mind foggy.

"That's nice. What about her?"

Then he kissed her eyes, lingering on each one.

"She said I shouldn't be so negative, that I should focus on the positive. My Gram said the same thing."

He kissed her, hard, their tongues pressing together,

her lips on fire. She didn't want to ever leave him, but there were still things that had to be discussed. Important things that she couldn't overlook.

"Is this positive enough for you?"

His room door opened behind him and he gently pulled her inside.

"Very positive. Still, what about our future? Will we have a future?"

The door began to close behind them. She stopped it with her foot.

"All I can say is that my AA meetings teach me to take it one day at a time. It's all we really have. One day, one moment, one breath at a time. I love you, Doctor Cori Parker, and on this one day, I want to make love to you. Neither one of us knows where it's going to lead. But for today, for tonight, let's love each other. When and if tomorrow comes, we'll deal with whatever happens. But for tonight, lie with me in my bed and I promise to love you with all my heart."

Cori knew firsthand about taking it a day at a time. She'd learned how to do that after her husband had died. Each day was a battle, but for Hailey's sake she'd managed to get through it. She'd done everything for Hailey, at the cost of putting her own needs and desires second. She'd lost control, wanting life to go a certain way so much that she'd almost caused her own accident with Hailey in the car.

So now she wanted to slow down and let life lead her wherever it may.

She took a deep breath and a couple steps backward. "There's something you should know."

"Can't it wait?" he asked moving toward her.

"No," she told him. "I have to tell you now."

He moved farther inside the room, letting go of her. She could leave if she wanted to, or stay. She knew he'd left it up to her.

He took a seat on the desk chair, while she stood by the door, still hesitant. She didn't know how long she would stay once she put it all out there, or if he'd still want her. She had some definite opinions about alcoholics and didn't know if she could change her mind.

She perched on the edge of the bed and continued. "My entire life changed in one moment, along with Hailey's. For a long time, I was afraid to drive at night, afraid that I'd meet the same fate as my husband. What would happen to Hailey then, if I died as well? Who would raise her? After more time passed, that fear turned into a loathing for anyone who had even one drink and got behind the wheel of a car. I became obsessed with forcing everyone around me to stop drinking anything remotely alcoholic. I'm sure everyone hated to be around me when I was behaving like that.

"Fortunately though, I finally accepted what had happened. That Jeremy was simply in the wrong place at the wrong time. It was an accident, and as long as people drive and drink, there'll be more accidents just like his, unfortunately. That's why I ran away from you that first night out on the street, before any of this got started. I couldn't believe I was falling for someone who abused alcohol."

"I'm not that person anymore," Gage said, his eyes moist. "I would never do anything to hurt you or Hailey. I made a decision today. I wanted a drink more than I've ever wanted one in my entire life. I needed that drink and told myself I deserved it. But when push came to shove, I didn't do it. I couldn't do it. I knew if I succumbed to the blissful high it most certainly would bring, obliterating all my guilt and self-doubt, I would never be sober again."

"Statistics aren't in your favor that you'll remain sober, and I couldn't take it if you started drinking again. I won't put myself or my daughter through that."

Gage gazed down at the floor, and then back at Cori. "All I can say is there are no guarantees in this life. You know that as well as I do. But if you'll give me a chance, I'll do my best to never take another drink. I can't lose you. I won't lose you."

They stared at each other for what seemed like forever. Cori trying to decide if she should trust this man with her heart, if his word was true, and if they could actually make it past that five-year mark. She wanted to discuss it some more, wanted to sit and have an open and honest conversation without sex being involved. She thought about how much good a cup of hot tea might do for them both.

Then, as if he could hear her thoughts, he said, "Let me get us a couple cups of tea and we can talk this over."

And as soon as he said it, she knew absolutely they could make it.

He stood and went for the door, but she stopped him.

"The tea can wait," she said.

Epilogue

One year later

Cori had cleared her patient schedule for the entire afternoon and intended to take full advantage of all the events at M & M Riding School, right outside of Briggs, Idaho, where Hailey and several of the other students would be demonstrating all that they'd learned over the past several months.

Not only had Hailey mastered proper Western riding form, but Helen Granger and the rest of her highly trained staff had taught Hailey all about horsemanship, including handling skills, control, and grooming and saddling her own horse. Cori's city-girl daughter was rapidly turning into a genuine cowgirl.

"All set, Mom," Hailey said while on horseback. Her daughter's best friend, Susan, rode up next to Hailey, along with Scout Granger, who had instantly befriended Hailey as soon as they'd met. They had become solid friends during the school year, and Hailey couldn't wait for Susan's visit so she and Scout could meet. Apparently they'd all hit it off, because the three girls had been inseparable over the past few weeks. And, much to everyone's delight, Susan's parents were seriously considering relocating from New York City to Briggs and buying the local sandwich shop, Deli Llama's, when the owners retired in the next few months.

Susan had spent most of the summer on the ranch and attended the riding school along with Hailey. Both girls had taken to riding as easily as riding a bike. They would spend their days helping out on the Circle R wherever they could, then going for long rides after their lessons at the school, with Scout leading the way. Most of the time, they'd be joined by the other Granger kids, Gavin and Joey, who more often than not would end up getting into some sort of a fix.

Fortunately, the girls seemed to be able to steer them in the right direction, avoiding calamity.

Still, Cori had to admit, the day Gavin decided to play rodeo clown with the Granger bull…well…she was just happy she'd only heard about how Hailey had saved him. They'd all been grounded for a week after that one, but that didn't seem to deter the boys' pranks.

Although, the more Cori got to know those boys, the more she thought their curiosity was to blame, rather than anything malicious.

Now as the boys rode up, along with their older brother, Buddy, who was going on thirteen, Cori felt both apprehension and genuine love for those two little rascals.

The school was less than a mile away if they headed up the back trail, or more than two miles if they chose to take the long way past the bull pen on the Granger land. The boys lived in the main house at M & M Riding School with their parents, Helen and Colt Granger, along with their half sister, Loran. They'd ridden over to escort the girls to the school, looking all cowboyed up in their best clothes and polished boots. Their grandpa, Dodge, was a stickler for proper manners and proper cowboy attire when the occasion warranted. And from the looks of those boys, their Western hats perched low on their foreheads, this graduation warranted their finest.

Most of the time, Cori could depend on Buddy to be the calm during the storm, but with the excitement everyone was feeling today, she could tell Buddy was just as antsy as the rest of the group to get this thing started.

"You kids take the back trail so I don't have to worry about any of you. I want your word on that one," Cori ordered, as she held up a hand to shield the sun from her eyes as she gazed up at Susan and Hailey. Her chocolate-colored cowgirl hat slipped back on her head, so she readjusted it lower on her forehead. The hat had become second nature to her now. She almost never left the house without it. Her hat and her boots had turned into a comfortable uniform she couldn't do without.

"You have my word," Buddy said in that baritone voice of his.

"Mine, too," everyone chimed in.

"Gage and I will be waiting for you, so don't make us worry."

They would be driving over as soon as everyone else was on their way.

"We won't, Doctor Remington," Gavin said, and they each turned their horses and took off for the back trail, with Hailey leading the way looking as if she'd grown up in that saddle. Not only had Hailey taken to living in the Teton Valley, but Cori had settled in and started her own geriatric practice within three months of moving to Briggs.

Once she'd arrived on the Circle R ranch, she had

fallen in love with it, just as her Gram had. There was no way either woman could ever return to their previous lives. Circle R and Briggs were now their home.

"I see the girls took off," Gage said as he walked up next to Cori, slipping his hand around her waist and pulling her in for a gentle kiss. His chest, arms and thighs had filled out from the continuous ranch work, and each time they touched he seemed a little stronger, his muscles seemed a little harder, as his resolve to make a life for his family never faltered. His gramps had been right. Gage was a natural cowboy and took to the lifestyle as easy as bees to honey.

"Yep, we're all set, and Buddy promised they would ride directly to the school," Cori told him once they separated.

"Then we better get going," Gage said. "We don't want to be late."

Gage and Cori walked up to where Buck was getting ready to mount Dark Night, his paint, who was probably as old as he was in horse years.

"You ready, Gramps?" Gage asked Buck as he took the reins from his grandfather.

"All set to go," Buck told Gage as he prepared himself to mount his favorite black stallion. Gage held the horse steady while Buck approached. He wore a crisp Western-style check shirt, a fringed suede vest, jeans, his well-worn boots and a brand-new dark chocolate–colored cowboy hat. He looked every bit the part of a great rancher and for the past two months had been looking forward to participating in the events today at the school. Not only had Helen Granger taught Hailey how to ride, but she'd found a way to get Buck back up on a horse after his hip had healed, a miracle in its own right.

"Let me help you," Cori told Buck, when he stood at the bottom of the three-step stool that allowed him to ride again. Once he was on horseback he could ride without a problem. It had been getting him up there that had proved to be the challenge, but he'd been working extra hard in the past few weeks and seemed to be a lot more limber.

"Don't need no help," Buck confirmed as he took the first two steps without a problem, then hesitated before he took the last one.

"Gramps," Gage said. "I know you can do this."

"You dang right I can," Gramps said. Then he moved onto the last stair, grabbed hold of the horn on the saddle and, in one smooth move, he stepped into the stirrup, hoisted a leg up over the stallion and eased himself down on the Western saddle that had been designed especially for him.

The horse took a few steps, but Gramps quickly had him under control.

"See you two there," Gramps said, looking satisfied with himself.

Cori and Gage watched as Gramps joined a few of his friends who wanted to escort him to the school. Everyone knew what an ordeal Buck had gone through to get back up on a horse, and as he approached they clapped and cheered his success.

"Who would have thought that man would be riding again?" Grandma May asked, as she rode up behind Cori and Gage. She wore brightly colored Western clothing and a white Western hat. Grandma May would be graduating along with the rest of the class at M & M today. Buck would have never agreed to attend the school if May hadn't asked for his help to learn how to ride properly. It was a little plan that she and Cori had cooked up to get Buck into that school. Fortunately for everyone, it had worked.

"I think we all did," Gage said, smiling up at her.

"It's his stubborn streak," May offered. "Keeps him young." She gave a little tug to the reins and rode off to join the rest of the group.

"Do you know how wonderful you are, Gage Remington?" Cori teased as they made their way toward the main ranch house. "You made this day happen. I've never seen either of our grandparents so happy."

"Thanks, but I'd be nothing if it wasn't for the incredible woman by my side, Doctor Cori Parker-Remington." He slipped his arms around her, and at once Cori felt the warmth of his love.

"And Hailey is in her glory, especially since you've been wearing the Sheriff badge she gave you last year."

"Every time I pin it on, it reminds me of my girls."

"All your girls?" Cori asked as she slipped her right hand over her ever-growing tummy. She was going on twenty-two weeks pregnant and her lower back had started feeling the weight of their baby girl, Jessie.

"All three of my girls," Gage said, turning to press his lips on Cori's. She never took his love for granted and seized the moment to show it with her warm kiss.

"I love you," he said, running his hand along her neck and tangling his fingers in her hair.

"I love you, with all my heart."

"With all my heart," he repeated. Then they resumed walking toward their white pickup truck, and Cori giggled with happiness as he helped her into the passenger seat.

"You should be riding over with everyone else," she told him, once he sat behind the wheel and turned over the ignition.

He shook his head no. "And let you drive there all alone? Never going to happen."

"I'm hardly alone," she said as an overzealous five-month-old Labrador Retriever licked her cheek, then sniffed her neck and gave out a little bark before he moved over to Gage and did the same.

Gage reached behind the seats and gave Zane some loving, and then he headed off the ranch toward the school.

"You know what?" she asked, while gazing at his beautiful profile, thinking of how happy he made her.

"No, what?"

"Out of all the cowboys I've read about in all of Zane Grey's books, you're my favorite."

"And why's that?"

"Because there's a double feature over at the Spud Drive-In and I can't think of a better way to spend the night than snuggled up with you and the girls in the back of this truck, munching on popcorn."

He laughed low in his throat. "Way ahead of you. Already bought the tickets, darlin'."

And with that, she leaned over and planted a kiss on her favorite cowboy's cheek.

* * * * *

If you liked this cowboy tale, pick up
these romances from
USA TODAY *bestselling author Mary Leo*

FALLING FOR THE COWBOY
AIMING FOR THE COWBOY
CHRISTMAS WITH THE RANCHER

Available now from Harlequin American Romance!

And don't miss the Christmas romance
coming next from Mary Leo,
Available December 2015!

From New York Times *bestselling author*
Jodi Thomas comes a sweeping new series set in a
remote west Texas town—where family can be made
by blood or by choice...

RANSOM CANYON
Available now from HQN Books.

Staten

WHEN HER OLD hall clock chimed eleven times, Staten Kirkland left Quinn O'Grady's bed. While she slept, he dressed in the shadows, watching her with only the light of the full moon. She'd given him what he needed tonight, and, as always, he felt as if he'd given her nothing.

Walking out to her porch, he studied the newly washed earth, thinking of how empty his life was except for these few hours he shared with Quinn. He'd never love her or anyone, but he wished he could do something for her. Thanks to hard work and inherited land, he was a rich man. She was making a go of her farm, but barely. He could help her if she'd let him. But he knew she'd never let him.

As he pulled on his boots, he thought of a dozen things he could do around the place. Like fixing that old tractor out in the mud or modernizing her irrigation system. The tractor had been sitting out by the road for months. If she'd accept his help, it wouldn't take him an hour to pull the old John Deere out and get the engine running again.

Only, she wouldn't accept anything from him. He knew better than to ask.

He wasn't even sure they were friends some days.

Maybe they were more. Maybe less. He looked down at his palm, remembering how she'd rubbed cream on it and worried that all they had in common was loss and the need, now and then, to touch another human being.

The screen door creaked. He turned as Quinn, wrapped in an old quilt, moved out into the night.

"I didn't mean to wake you," he said as she tiptoed across the snow-dusted porch. "I need to get back. Got eighty new yearlings coming in early." He never apologized for leaving, and he wasn't now. He was simply stating facts. With the cattle rustling going on and his plan to enlarge his herd, he might have to hire more men. As always, he felt as though he needed to be on his land and on alert.

She nodded and moved to stand in front of him.

Staten waited. They never touched after they made love. He usually left without a word, but tonight she obviously had something she wanted to say.

Another thing he probably did wrong, he thought. He never complimented her, never kissed her on the mouth, never said any words after he touched her. If she didn't make little sounds of pleasure now and then, he wouldn't have been sure he satisfied her.

Now, standing so close to her, he felt more a stranger than a lover. He knew the smell of her skin, but he had no idea what she was thinking most of the time. She knew quilting and how to make soap from her lavender. She played the piano like an angel and didn't even own a TV. He knew ranching and watched from his recliner every game the Dallas Cowboys played.

If they ever spent over an hour talking they'd probably figure out they had nothing in common. He'd played every sport in high school, and she'd played in both the orchestra and the band. He'd collected most of his college hours online, and she'd gone all the way to New York to school. But they'd loved the same person. Amalah had been Quinn's best friend and his one love. Only, they rarely talked about how they felt. Not anymore. Not ever really. It was too painful, he guessed, for both of them.

Tonight the air was so still, moisture hung like invisible lace. She looked to be closer to her twenties than her forties. Quinn had her own quiet kind of beauty. She always had, and he guessed she still would even when she was old.

To his surprise, she leaned in and kissed his mouth.

He watched her. "You want more?" he finally asked, figuring it was probably the dumbest thing to say to a naked woman standing two inches away from him. He had no idea what *more* would be. They always had sex once, if they had it at all, when he knocked on her door. Sometimes neither made the first move, and they just cuddled on the couch and held each other. Quinn wasn't a passionate woman. What they did was just satisfying a need that they both had now and then.

She kissed him again without saying a word. When her cheek brushed against his stubbled chin, it was wet and tasted newborn like the rain.

Slowly, Staten moved his hands under her blanket and circled her warm body, then he pulled her closer and kissed her fully like he hadn't kissed a woman since his wife died.

Her lips were soft and inviting. When he opened her mouth and invaded, it felt far more intimate than anything they had ever done, but he didn't stop. She wanted this from him, and he had no intention of denying her.

No one would ever know that she was the thread that kept him together some days.

When he finally broke the kiss, Quinn was out of breath. She pressed her forehead against his jaw and he waited.

"From now on," she whispered so low he felt her words more than heard them, "when you come to see me, I need you to kiss me goodbye before you go. If I'm asleep, wake me. You don't have to say a word, but you have to kiss me."

She'd never asked him for anything. He had no intention of saying no. His hand spread across the small of her back and pulled her hard against him. "I won't forget if that's what you want." He could feel her heart pounding and knew her asking had not come easy.

She nodded. "It's what I want."

He brushed his lips over hers, loving the way she sighed as if wanting more before she pulled away.

"Good night," she said as though rationing pleasure. Stepping inside, she closed the screen door between them.

Raking his hair back, he put on his hat as he watched her fade into the shadows. The need to return was already building in him. "I'll be back Friday night if it's all right. It'll be late, I've got to visit with my grandmother and do her list of chores before I'll be free. If you like, I could bring barbecue for supper?" He felt as if he was rambling, but something needed to be said, and he had no idea what.

"And vegetables," she suggested.

He nodded. She wanted a meal, not just the meat. "I'll have them toss in sweet potato fries and okra."

She held the blanket tight as if he might see her body.

She didn't meet his eyes when he added, "I enjoyed kissing you, Quinn. I look forward to doing so again."

With her head down, she nodded as she vanished into the darkness without a word.

He walked off the porch, deciding if he lived to be a hundred he'd never understand Quinn. As far as he knew, she'd never had a boyfriend when they were in school. And his wife had never told him about Quinn dating anyone special when she went to New York to that fancy music school. Now, in her forties, she'd never had a date, much less a lover that he knew of. But she hadn't been a virgin when they'd made love the first time.

Asking her about her love life seemed far too personal a question.

Climbing into his truck, he forced his thoughts toward problems at the ranch. He needed to hire men; they'd lost three cattle to rustlers this month. As he planned the coming day, Staten did what he always did: he pushed Quinn to a corner of his mind, where she'd wait until he saw her again.

As he passed through the little town of Crossroads, all the businesses were closed up tight except for a gas station that stayed open twenty-four hours to handle the few travelers needing to refuel or brave enough to sample their food.

Half a block away from the station was his grandmother's bungalow, dark amid the cluster of senior citizens' homes. One huge light in the middle of all the little homes shone a low glow on to the porch of each house. The tiny white cottages reminded him of a circle of wagons camped just off the main road. She'd lived fifty years on Kirkland land, but when Staten's granddad, her husband, had died, she'd wanted to move to town. She'd been a teacher in her early years and said she needed to be with her friends in the retirement community, not alone in the big house on the ranch.

He swore without anger, remembering all her instructions the day she moved to town. She wanted her only grandson to drop by every week to switch out batteries, screw in lightbulbs and reprogram the TV that she'd spent the week messing up. He didn't mind dropping by. Besides his father, who considered his home—when he wasn't in Washington—to be Dallas, Granny was the only family Staten had.

A quarter mile past the one main street of Crossroads, his truck lights flashed across four teenagers walking along the road between the Catholic church and the gas station.

Three boys and a girl. Fifteen or sixteen, Staten guessed.

For a moment the memory of Randall came to mind. He'd been about their age when he'd crashed, and he'd worn the same type of blue-and-white letter jacket that two of the boys wore tonight.

Staten slowed as he passed them. "You kids need a ride?" The lights were still on at the church, and a few cars were in the parking lot. Saturday night, Staten remembered. Members of 4-H would probably be working in the basement on projects.

One kid waved. A tall Hispanic boy named Lucas, whom he thought was the oldest son of the head wrangler on the Collins Ranch. Reyes was his last name, and Staten remembered the boy being one of a dozen young kids who were often hired part-time at the ranch.

Staten had heard the kid was almost as good a wrangler as his father. The magic of working with horses must have been passed down from father to son, along with the height. Young Reyes might be lean but, thanks to working, he would be in better shape than either of the football boys. When Lucas Reyes finished high school, he'd have no trouble hiring on at any of the big ranches, including the Double K.

"No, we're fine, Mr. Kirkland," the Reyes boy said politely. "We're just walking down to the station for a Coke. Reid Collins's brother is picking us up soon."

"No crime in that, mister," a redheaded kid in a letter jacket answered. His words came fast and clipped, reminding Staten of how his son had sounded.

Volume from a boy trying to prove he was a man, Staten thought.

He couldn't see the faces of the two boys with letter jackets, but the girl kept her head up. "We've been working on a project for the fair," she answered politely. "I'm Lauren Brigman, Mr. Kirkland."

Staten nodded. *Sheriff Brigman's daughter, I remember you.* She knew enough to be polite, but it was none of his business. "Good evening, Lauren," he said. "Nice to see you again. Good luck with the project."

When he pulled away, he shook his head. Normally, he wouldn't have bothered to stop. This might be small-town Texas, but they were not his problem. If he saw the Reyes boy again, he would apologize.

Staten swore. At this rate he'd turn into a nosy old man by forty-five. It didn't seem that long ago that he and Amalah used to walk up to the gas station after meetings at the church.

Hell, maybe Quinn asking to kiss him had rattled him more than he thought. He needed to get his head straight. She was just a friend. A woman he turned to when the storms came. Nothing more. That was the way they both wanted it.

Until he made it back to her porch next Friday night, he had a truckload of trouble at the ranch to worry about.

Lauren

A MIDNIGHT MOON blinked its way between storm clouds as Lauren Brigman cleaned the mud off her shoes. The guys had gone inside the gas station for Cokes. She didn't really want anything to drink, but it was either walk over with the others after working on their fair projects or stay back at the church and talk to Mrs. Patterson.

Somewhere Mrs. Patterson had gotten the idea that since Lauren didn't have a mother around, she should take every opportunity to have a "girl talk" with the sheriff's daughter.

Lauren wanted to tell the old woman that she had known all the facts of life by the age of seven, and she really did not need a buddy to share her teenage years with. Besides, her mother lived in Dallas. It wasn't like she'd died. She'd just left. Just because she couldn't stand the sight of Lauren's dad didn't mean she didn't call and talk to Lauren almost every week. Maybe Mom had just gotten tired of the sheriff's nightly lectures. Lauren had heard every one of Pop's talks so many times that she had them memorized in alphabetical order.

Her grades put her at the top of the sophomore class, and she saw herself bound for college in less than three years. Lauren had no intention of getting pregnant, or doing drugs, or any of the other fearful situations Mrs. Patterson and her father had hinted might befall her. Her pop didn't even want her dating until she was sixteen, and, judging from the boys she knew in high school, she'd just as soon go dateless until eighteen. Maybe college would have better pickings. Some of these guys were so dumb she was surprised they got their cowboy hats on straight every morning.

Reid Collins walked out from the gas station first with a can of Coke in each hand. "I bought you one even though you said you didn't want anything to drink," he announced as he neared. "Want to lean on me while you clean your shoes?"

Lauren rolled her eyes. Since he'd grown a few inches and started working out, Reid thought he was God's gift to girls.

"Why?" she asked as she tossed the stick. "I have a brick wall to lean on. And don't get any ideas we're on a date, Reid, just because I walked over here with you."

"I don't date sophomores," he snapped. "I'm on first string, you know. I could probably date any senior I want to. Besides, you're like a little sister, Lauren. We've known each other since you were in the first grade."

She thought of mentioning that playing first string on a football team that only had forty players total, including the coaches and water boy, wasn't any great accomplishment, but arguing with Reid would rot her brain. He'd been born rich, and he'd thought he knew everything since he'd cleared the birth canal. She feared his disease was terminal.

"If you're cold, I'll let you wear my football jacket."

When she didn't comment, he bragged, "I had to reorder a bigger size after a month of working out."

She hated to, but if she didn't compliment him soon, he'd never stop begging. "You look great in the jacket, Reid. Half the seniors on the team aren't as big as you." There was nothing wrong with Reid from the neck down. In a few years he'd be a knockout with the Collins good looks and trademark rusty hair, not quite brown, not quite red. But he still wouldn't interest her.

"So, when I get my driver's license next month, do you want to take a ride?"

Lauren laughed. "You've been asking that since I was in the third grade and you got your first bike. The answer is still no. We're friends, Reid. We'll always be friends, I'm guessing."

He smiled a smile that looked as if he'd been practicing. "I know, Lauren, but I keep wanting to give you a chance now and then. You know, some guys don't want to date the sheriff's daughter, and I hate to point it out, babe, but if you don't fill out some, it's going to be bad news in college." He had the nerve to point at her chest.

"I know." She managed to pull off a sad look. "Having my father is a cross I have to bear. Half the guys in town are afraid of him. Like he might arrest them for talking to me. Which he might." She had no intention of discussing her lack of curves with Reid.

"No, it's not fear of him, exactly," Reid corrected. "I think it's more the bullet holes they're afraid of. Every time a guy looks at you, your old man starts patting his service weapon. Nerve-racking habit, if you ask me. From the looks of it, I seem to be the only one he'll let stand beside you, and that's just because our dads are friends."

She grinned. Reid was spoiled and conceited and self-centered, but he was right. They'd probably always be friends. Her dad was the sheriff, and his was the mayor of Crossroads, even though he lived five miles from town on one of the first ranches established near Ransom Canyon.

With her luck, Reid would be the only guy in the state that her father would let her date. Grumpy old Pop had what she called Terminal Cop Disease. Her father thought everyone, except his few friends, was most likely a criminal, anyone under thirty should be stopped and searched, and anyone who'd ever smoked pot could not be trusted.

Tim O'Grady, Reid's eternal shadow, walked out of the station with a huge frozen drink. The clear cup showed off its red-and-yellow layers of cherry-and-pineapple-flavored sugar.

Where Reid was balanced in his build, Tim was lanky, disjointed. He seemed to be made of mismatched parts. His arms were too long. His feet seemed too big, and his wired smile barely fit in his mouth. When he took a deep draw on his drink, he staggered and held his forehead from the brain freeze.

Lauren laughed as he danced around like a puppet with his strings crossed. Timothy, as the teachers called him, was always good for a laugh. He had the depth of cheap paint but the imagination of a natural-born storyteller.

"Maybe I shouldn't have gotten an icy drink on such a cold night," he mumbled between gulps. "If I freeze from the inside out, put me up on Main Street as a statue."

Lauren giggled.

Lucas Reyes was the last of their small group to come outside. Lucas hadn't bought anything, but he evidently was avoiding standing outside with her. She'd known Lucas Reyes for a few years, maybe longer, but he never talked to her. Like Reid and Tim, he was a year ahead of her, but since he rarely talked, she usually only noticed him as a background person in her world.

Unlike them, Lucas didn't have a family name following him around opening doors for a hundred miles.

They all four lived east of Crossroads along the rambling canyon called Ransom Canyon. Lauren and her father lived in one of a cluster of houses near the lake, as did Tim's parents. Reid's family ranch was five miles farther out. She had no idea where Lucas's family lived. Maybe on the Collins Ranch. His father worked on the Bar W, which had been in the Collins family for over a hundred years. The area around the headquarters looked like a small village.

Reid repeated the plan. "My brother said he'd drop Sharon off and be back for us. But if they get busy doing their thing it could be an hour. We might as well walk back and sit on the church steps."

"Great fun," Tim complained. "Everything's closed. It's freezing out here, and I swear this town is so dead somebody should bury it."

"We could start walking toward home," Lauren suggested as she pulled a tiny flashlight from her key chain. The canyon lake wasn't more than a mile. If they walked they wouldn't be so cold. She could probably be home before Reid's dumb brother could get his lips off Sharon. If rumors were true, Sharon had very kissable lips, among other body parts.

"Better than standing around here," Reid said as Tim

kicked mud toward the building. "I'd rather be walking than sitting. Plus, if we go back to the church, Mrs. Patterson will probably come out to keep us company."

Without a vote, they started walking. Lauren didn't like the idea of stumbling into mud holes now covered up by a dusting of snow along the side of the road, but it sounded better than standing out front of the gas station. Besides, the moon offered enough light, making the tiny flashlight her father insisted she carry worthless.

Within a few yards, Reid and Tim had fallen behind and were lighting up a smoke. To her surprise, Lucas stayed beside her.

"You don't smoke?" she asked, not really expecting him to answer.

"No, can't afford the habit," he said, surprising her. "I've got plans, and they don't include lung cancer."

Maybe the dark night made it easier to talk, or maybe Lauren didn't want to feel so alone in the shadows. "I was starting to think you were a mute. We've had a few classes together, and you've never said a word. Even tonight you were the only one who didn't talk about your project."

Lucas shrugged. "Didn't see the point. I'm just entering for the prize money, not trying to save the world or build a better tomorrow."

She giggled.

He laughed, too, realizing he'd just made fun of the whole point of the projects. "Plus," he added, "there's just not much opportunity to get a word in around those two." He nodded his head at the two letter jackets falling farther behind as a cloud of smoke haloed above them.

She saw his point. The pair trailed them by maybe

twenty feet or more, and both were talking about football. Neither seemed to require a listener.

"Why do you hang out with them?" she asked. Lucas didn't seem to fit. Studious and quiet, he hadn't gone out for sports or joined many clubs that she knew about. "Jocks usually hang out together."

"I wanted to work on my project tonight, and Reid offered me a ride. Listening to football talk beats walking in this weather."

Lauren tripped into a pothole. Lucas's hand shot out and caught her in the darkness. He steadied her, then let go.

"Thanks. You saved my life," she joked.

"Hardly, but if I had, you'd owe me a blood debt."

"Would I have to pay?"

"Of course. It would be a point of honor. You'd have to save me or be doomed to a coward's hell."

"Lucky you just kept me from tripping, or I'd be following you around for years waiting to repay the debt." She rubbed her arm where he'd touched her. He was stronger than she'd thought he would be. "You lift weights?"

The soft laughter came again. "Yeah, it's called work. Until I was sixteen, I spent the summers and every weekend working on Reid's father's ranch. Once I was old enough, I signed up at the Kirkland place to cowboy when they need extras. Every dime I make is going to college tuition in a year. That's why I don't have a car yet. When I get to college, I won't need it, and the money will go toward books."

"But you're just a junior. You've still got a year and a half of high school."

"I've got it worked out so I can graduate early. High

school's a waste of time. I've got plans. I can make a hundred-fifty a day working, and my dad says he thinks I'll be able to cowboy every day I'm not in school this spring and all summer."

She tripped again, and his hand steadied her once more. Maybe it was her imagination, but she swore he held on a little longer than necessary.

"You're an interesting guy, Lucas Reyes."

"I will be," he said. "Once I'm in college, I can still come home and work breaks and weekends. I'm thinking I can take a few online classes during the summer, live at home and save enough to pay for the next year. I'm going to Tech no matter what it takes."

"You planning on getting through college in three years, too?"

He shook his head. "Don't know if I can. But I'll have the degree, whatever it is, before I'm twenty-two."

No one her age had ever talked of the future like that. Like they were just passing through this time in their life and something yet to come mattered far more. "When you are somebody, I think I'd like to be your friend."

"I hope we will be more than that, Lauren." His words were so low, she wasn't sure she heard them.

"Hey, you two deadbeats up there!" Reid yelled. "I got an idea."

Lauren didn't want the conversation with Lucas to end, but if she ignored Reid he'd just get louder. "What?"

Reid ran up between them and put an arm over both her and Lucas's shoulders. "How about we break into the Gypsy House? I hear it's haunted by Gypsies who died a hundred years ago."

Tim caught up to them. As always, he agreed with Reid. "Look over there in the trees. The place is just waiting for us. Heard if you rattle a Gypsy's bones, the dead will speak to you." Tim's eyes glowed in the moonlight. "I had a cousin once who said he heard voices in that old place, and no one was there but him."

"This is not a good idea." Lauren tried to back away, but Reid held her shoulder tight.

"Come on, Lauren, for once in your life, do something that's not safe. No one's lived in the old place for years. How much trouble can we get into?"

Tim's imagination had gone wild. According to him all kinds of things could happen. They might find a body. Ghosts could run them out, or the spirit of a Gypsy might take over their minds. Who knew, zombies might sleep in the rubble of old houses.

Lauren rolled her eyes. She didn't want to think of the zombies getting Tim. A walking dead with braces was too much.

"It's just a rotting old house," Lucas said so low no one heard but Lauren. "There's probably rats or rotten floors. It's an accident waiting to happen. How about you come back in the daylight, Reid, if you really want to explore the place?"

"We're all going, now," Reid announced, as he shoved Lauren off the road and into the trees that blocked the view of the old homestead from passing cars. "Think of the story we'll have to tell everyone Monday. We will have explored a haunted house and lived to tell the tale."

Reason told her to protest more strongly, but at fifteen, reason wasn't as intense as the possibility of an adventure. Just once, she'd have a story to tell. Just this once…her father wouldn't find out.

They rattled across the rotting porch steps fighting tumbleweeds that stood like flimsy guards around the place. The door was locked and boarded up. The smell of decay hung in the foggy air, and a tree branch scraped against one side of the house as if whispering for them to stay back.

The old place didn't look like much. It might have been the remains of an early settlement, built solid to face the winters with no style or charm. Odds were, Gypsies never even lived in it. It appeared to be a half dugout with a second floor built on years later. The first floor was planted down into the earth a few feet, so the second-floor windows were just above their heads, giving the place the look of a house that had been stepped on by a giant.

Everyone called it the Gypsy House because a group of hippies had squatted there in the seventies. They'd painted a peace sign on one wall, but it had faded and been rained on until it almost looked like a witching sign. No one remembered when the hippies had moved on or who owned the house now, but somewhere in its past a family named Stanley must have lived there because old-timers called it the Stanley house.

"I heard devil worshippers lived here years ago." Tim began making scary-movie-soundtrack noises. "Body parts are probably scattered in the basement. They say once Satan moves in, only the blood of a virgin will wash the place clean."

Reid's laughter sounded nervous. "That leaves me out."

Tim jabbed his friend. "You wish. I say you'll be the

first to scream when a dead hand, not connected to a body, touches you."

"Shut up, Tim." Reid's uneasy voice echoed in the night. "You're freaking me out. Besides, there is no basement. It's just a half dugout built into the ground, so we'll find no buried bodies."

Lauren screamed as Reid kicked a low window in, and all the guys laughed.

"You go first, Lucas," Reid ordered. "I'll stand guard."

To Lauren's surprise, Lucas slipped into the space. His feet hit the ground with a thud somewhere in the blackness.

"You next, Tim," Reid announced as if he were the commander.

"Nope. I'll go after you." All Tim's laughter had disappeared. Apparently he'd frightened himself.

"I'll go." Lauren suddenly wanted this entire adventure to be over with. With her luck, animals were wintering in the old place.

"I'll help you down." Reid lowered her into the window space.

As she moved through total darkness, her feet wouldn't quite touch the bottom. For a moment she just hung, afraid to tell Reid to drop her.

Then she felt Lucas's hands at her waist. Slowly he took her weight.

"I'm in," she called back to Reid. He let her hands go, and she dropped against Lucas.

"You all right?" Lucas whispered near her hair.

"This was a dumb idea."

She felt him laugh more than she heard it. "That you talking or the Gypsy's advice? Of all the brains dropping in here tonight, yours would probably be the most interesting to take over, so watch out. A ghost might just climb in your head and let free all the secret thoughts you keep inside, Lauren."

He pulled her a foot into the blackness as a letter jacket dropped through the window. His hands circled her waist. She could feel him breathing as Reid finally landed, cussing the darkness. For a moment it seemed all right for Lucas to stay close; then in a blink, he was gone from her side.

Now the tiny flashlight offered Lauren some much-needed light. The house was empty except for an old wire bed frame and a few broken stools. With Reid in the lead, they moved up rickety stairs to the second floor, where shadowy light came from big dirty windows.

Tim hesitated when the floor's boards began to rock as if the entire second story were on some kind of see-saw. He backed down the steps a few feet, letting the others go first. "I don't know if this second story will hold us all." Fear rattled in his voice.

Reid laughed and teased Tim as he stomped across the second floor, making the entire room buck and pitch. "Come on up, Tim. This place is better than a fun house."

Stepping hesitantly on the upstairs floor, Lauren felt Lucas just behind her and knew he was watching over her.

Tim dropped down a few more steps, not wanting to even try.

Lucas backed against the wall between the windows, his hand still brushing Lauren's waist to keep her steady as Reid jumped to make the floor shake. The whole house seemed to moan in pain, like a hundred-year-old man standing up one arthritic joint at a time.

When Reid yelled for Tim to join them, Tim started back up the broken stairs, just before the second floor buckled and crumbled. Tim dropped out of sight as rotten lumber pinned him halfway between floors.

His scream of pain ended Reid's laughter.

In a blink, dust and boards flew as pieces of the roof rained down on them and the second floor vanished below them, board by rotting board.

REQUEST YOUR FREE BOOKS!
2 FREE NOVELS PLUS 2 FREE GIFTS!

She'd know that butt anywhere. Hunter Boone.

In eleven years, his derriere hadn't changed much. And,
apparently, the view still managed to take her breath away.

"Need some help with that, Josie?" Her father's voice
made her wince.

She was clutching a tray of her dad's famous German
breakfast kolaches and hiding behind the display counter.
Why was she—a rational, professional woman—ducking
behind a bakery counter? Because *he'd* walked in.

She shot her father a look as she said, "Thanks, Dad.
I've got it." Taking a deep breath, she stood slowly and
slid the tray into the display cabinet with care.

"Josie? Josie Stephens?" a high-pitched voice asked.
"Oh my God, look at you. Why, you haven't changed
since high school."

Josie glanced at the woman but couldn't place her, so
she smiled and said, "Thanks. You, too."

That was when her gaze wandered to Hunter. He was
waiting. And, from the look on his face, he *knew* Josie
had no idea who the woman was.

"So it's true?" the woman continued. "Your dad said you were coming to help him, but I couldn't imagine you back *here*. We *all* know how much you hated Stonewall Crossing." Josie remembered her then. Winnie Michaels. "What did you call it, redneck hell—right?" Winnie kept going, teasing—but with a definite edge. "Guess hell froze over."

"Kind of hard to say no when your dad needs you," Josie answered, forcing herself not to snap.

Her father jumped to her defense. "She wasn't about to let her old man try to run this place on his own."

"It's kinda weird to see the two of you standing here." Winnie glanced back and forth between Josie and Hunter. "I mean, without having your tongues down each other's throats and all."

Hunter wasn't smiling anymore. "I've gotta get these to the boys."

Josie saw him take the huge box by the register. A swift kick of disappointment prompted her to blurt out, "Too bad, Hunter. If I remember it correctly, you knew how to kiss a girl."

"If you remember? Ouch." His eyes swept her face, lingering on her lips. "Have fun while you're back in hell, Jo. I'll see you around."

Don't miss
A COWBOY'S CHRISTMAS REUNION
by Sasha Summers,
available in October 2015 wherever
Harlequin® American Romance®
books and ebooks are sold.

www.Harlequin.com

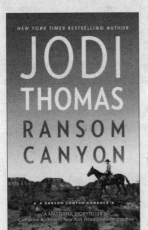

Turn your love of reading into rewards you'll love with
Harlequin My Rewards

**Join for FREE today at
www.HarlequinMyRewards.com**

Earn **FREE BOOKS** of your choice.

Experience **EXCLUSIVE OFFERS** and contests.

Enjoy **BOOK RECOMMENDATIONS**
selected just for you.

PLUS! Sign up now
and get **500** points
right away!

Earn
FREE
REWARDS
HarlequinMyRewards.com
Join
Today!

MYR16R